SECOND CHANCES

EMMA LEIGH REED

Emma Leigh Reed

Copyright © 2015 by Emma Leigh Reed

Warning: The unauthorized reproduction or distribution of this copyrighted work is illegal. Criminal copyright infringement, including infringement without monetary gain, is investigated by the FBI and is punishable by up to 5 (five) years in federal prison and a fine of $250,000.

Names, characters and incidents depicted in this book are products of the author's imagination or are used fictitiously. Any resemblance to actual events, locales, organizations, or persons, living or dead, is entirely coincidental and beyond the intent of the author or the publisher.

No part of this book may be reproduced or transmitted in any form or by any means, electronic or mechanical, including photocopying, recording, or by any information storage and retrieval system, without permission in writing from the publisher.

To my children: Alexa-for teaching me by example how to step out of my comfort zone; Rachel-for proofreading everything and never letting me give up; Nathan-you have taught me to view the world so differently.

Chapter 1

Kira Nichols pushed back her shoulder length light brown hair as the crisp salt air blew it across her face. As she walked up the path to the cul-de-sac, her sneakers left small impressions in the soft sand.

She sprang into a run when she heard the rumble of a sports car that was going too fast for a street where small children liked to play. She arrived at the cul-de-sac just as the vehicle skidded to a stop in front of the empty lot across from her house. Then she caught her breath as a lean man with rugged features got out of the car. He flashed her a smile that probably caused most women to melt at his feet.

As the man moved across the lot toward the foundation, which had been capped over and abandoned for about a year now, Kira squared her shoulders and approached him. He was at least six feet tall, and she felt minute beside him. She willed herself to appear calm, but she could feel her cheeks begin to flush.

"Grant Rutledge." He paused and extended his hand to her. His deep voice, like a shot of brandy, was warm and soothing. She swallowed hard, her anger at his reckless driving temporarily forgotten. Then it flared back, and she ignored his hand.

"Do you know there are children in this area?" she demanded, planting her hands on her hips.

"My apologies if you felt I was going too fast." He gave an exaggerated glance around. "There aren't any children about now."

He offered that smile again, and in spite of her anger, her heart softened for a moment. His hand was still extended, so she shook his calloused fingers. Tingles shot up her arm, and she struggled to keep herself from yanking her hand away. Heat flooded her face. She prayed he couldn't tell.

"Again, I apologize. I hope you won't think I have no regard for children."

Kira turned to go. She gestured absently at his car and said, "I just know the type."

As she forced herself to walk slowly toward her house, she could feel his eyes on her back. She felt both foolish and thankful that she had stayed in shape.

The solitude of the cul-de-sac was one of the reasons she had always loved this spot as a child whenever she had visited her grandfather. Her house, which she had inherited from him, had been the only one in this two-lot area for years, but it looked like they were going to pick up the pace across the street again. She hoped the new construction company would limit their work to business hours, particularly the hours when Jared would be in preschool.

She thought back to the long hours the last group of workers had kept when they put in the foundation. Jared had been unable to sleep due to the noise and disruption of his routine. Hopefully this time around the noise wouldn't disturb him. He was just beginning to sleep through the night.

If only she could.

* * *

Jared ran up the walkway to meet Kira, signing furiously: "Who is that man?"

"That is Grant Rutledge," she signed back. "He is going to be building the new house, so you will need to stay away from the construction site."

Jared's hands and fingers flew in his excitement to know about the new house, and the fast car he could see parked next to the lot.

"Jared, use your words." Kira ushered him into the house.

"Car, red."

"Yes, the car was red, and it's very fast, so you must stay away from there."

Barbara, her housekeeper, joined them in the hall. Kira met Barbara's eyes over Jared's head and gave her the "I have so much to tell you" look.

"Time to get ready for the day, Jared," Barbara interjected.

Jared skipped off to the bedroom happily, and Barbara handed Kira a cup of coffee.

"Spill. I saw him. It wasn't the fast car that made you come into this house so quickly."

Kira walked slowly to the sliding doors, which overlooked the ocean. "What happened to the quietness of our lives? Why do I feel like it is gone?"

"Is it gone?" Barbara asked. "Or just stirred up a little?"

Barbara had been one of Kira's strongest supporters after Patrick's fatal car accident four years ago, when Jared was just six months old. She said, "I think maybe you've been holding on to grief and bitterness for so long that you don't have any idea how to look objectively at life."

"But—"

"But nothing, Kira. Jared needs you, yes. But you can't build your whole life around him. That's not good for either of you.

"Barb, it's not like that."

"Honey, you've been holding on for so long. You know I'm angry with Patrick too. He was Jared's father. He should have been here right beside you. But you need to take care of yourself now, too."

"Stop! We are not going to rehash that night, and we certainly aren't going to blame Patrick. He's gone, and nothing is going to change that."

Kira took a deep breath and looked toward the ocean. For a moment she was able to release the weight of the here and now and simply follow the calming movement of the waves.

Then something caught Kira's eye, and she turned to see Grant taking measurements at the empty lot. Her emotions stirred as she watched his dark, wavy hair blow in the breeze. Half sighing, half growling to herself, she turned from the window. Distractions were not what she needed now. There was a routine to follow. For Jared's sake.

* * *

Putting in a day's preparation work around the construction site, Grant realized how much he had missed the hands-on elements of this business. It felt good to be home.

He could've done without the distraction this morning, though. His new neighbor—Kira Nichols. He had made a few phone calls, but no one seemed to know very much about her. A very private person, apparently. Even so, he had caught himself wondering about her throughout the day.

Later, as he walked back to his car to drive to dinner with his parents, he looked over at her house, hoping to catch another glimpse of those stormy eyes before he headed out. No such luck. He shook his head, got into his MG, and headed for his parents' homestead.

One of the best parts of moving back to Maine from Texas was the chance to join in family gatherings again. As he walked into his parents' front hallway, the aroma of baking bread coming from the kitchen assaulted his senses. He inhaled deeply. As a child, his trips to the kitchen were often rewarded with cookies and home-baked sweets. Maybe that still was possible.

Mary Lou, Grant's mom, was singing and dancing as she moved around the kitchen, pausing frequently to stir the gravy on the stovetop. As Grant watched, she bent down to look in the oven, still humming to herself. Grant crossed the kitchen floor and kissed her on the cheek as he snagged a roll from the counter.

"Hi, Mom."

"I saw that, Grant," Mary Lou said. She laughed. "I'm glad you decided to come over tonight for dinner. We don't seem to see you often enough."

"Wouldn't miss your cooking for the world."

"Make yourself useful then." She handed him a spoon. "Start stirring that gravy so it doesn't burn." Then she called to one of his brothers, who were in the next room. "Samuel, come set the table."

The kitchen was suddenly abuzz with the hustle and bustle. Sam set the table while Grant stirred the gravy. Mary Lou sliced roast beef and then piled carrots, potatoes, and onions on a platter and brought it to the table.

"Brandon and Marcus, dinnertime. It's ready and getting cold," Mary Lou yelled. "Grant, go track down your brother and your father."

As the family gathered around the table for dinner, Grant's father directed the conversation to how the construction was starting. Although Marcus was semi-retired, Grant knew that he was itching to be back on the site with hammer in hand to lead his sons as they raised the walls and roofs.

"Friday is wall raising, Dad," Grant said. "We can use a fourth hand, and I know you are dying to spend at least one day there."

Marcus, with a twinkle in his eyes, winked at Mary Lou and said, "I'll be there."

"You just made your father's night." Mary Lou smiled at Marcus. "Isn't this the site next to Kira Nichols' home?"

"Yes. Do you know her?" Grant was pleased that the conversation has made a turn toward Kira without his help.

"I know her housekeeper, Barbara. We attended Kira's husband's funeral four years ago, but we don't know Kira that well."

"How'd her husband die?"

"He was in a car accident, I believe. Her son was just a baby then."

Grant absorbed the information his mother freely gave. He left his food on his plate untouched while his mind raced with unanswered questions.

"Someone told me that her son is disabled. What's wrong with him?"

"I'm not sure. I hardly ever see Barbara. I know Jared cried a lot as an infant, and then he never really talked. At that time they were struggling to figure out exactly what his problem was. I guess if you're that interested, you will have to ask Kira directly."

Pushing back his chair, Grant started to clear the table. "That's probably not the best idea. I met her today, and

I'm not sure we got off on the right foot. She seems quite standoffish and very private."

In the kitchen, Grant started the dishes, his mind filled with thoughts of Kira and her son. She seemed like an awfully young person to have gone through so much heartache already.

Shaking his head, Grant turned his attention to the dishes. He really didn't need to be thinking about any of this. He had moved back to town to take over the family business. He didn't need any distractions in his life right now, certainly not a single mom with a disabled child, regardless of how attractive she was.

She was attractive, though. And spunky. She had put him in his place the minute she saw him driving too quickly for that area. Grant smiled to himself. Yes, he was certain he'd felt some chemistry.

"What's got you grinning?"

Grant turned to see Brandon and Sam standing there watching him.

"Was I grinning?" he asked.

"Oh, yeah. What gives?" Brandon said.

"Nothing. Just thinking."

"Not buying it, bro. Just because I'm the youngest doesn't mean you can pull the wool over my eyes," Brandon said.

"Did ya' meet some woman and you're holding out on us?" Sam teased.

Grant laughed. "Not likely. Now grab a towel and start drying before Mom sees that the dishes aren't done."

Finishing the dishes, Grant enjoyed the banter with his younger brothers. An hour later, after saying goodnight to his parents, Grant started for his apartment.

Once he was back in the MG, his thoughts once again turned toward Kira. She was a petite thing, maybe five two, but definitely full of moxie. He smiled to himself. Her tenacity had sparked a challenge to him. He wondered when he would see her next.

Chapter 2

"Barbara, I'm going to take Jared down to the beach today," Kira said the next morning. "I want him to tolerate the water, and it will be good for him to try to get used to the gritty wet sand a little bit at a time."

"Do you think he's up for it now?" Barbara asked. She knew that after one disastrous trip, Kira had not taken Jared down to the ocean for a few months.

"I hope so," Kira said. She yawned behind her hand. "We'll do sensory therapy here first, which should help him stay focused on the beach."

Jared came in and sat at the table, ready for breakfast.

"Hi, honey," Kira said. "Here's your cereal. When you're through, I'll take you down to the beach. Maybe we'll find some great shells."

Signing no, Jared shook his head. Kira noticed that he was not making eye contact—a sure sign that he was a little bit off today. He hadn't slept well. The wrinkles on the bed sheets often disturbed him, and Kira had gotten up repeatedly to try to soothe him. By two in the morning she had felt frustrated and snappy. Now Jared's eyes were glassy, and he stared into space. He rocked gently forward and back in his chair.

"I'll pack some snacks to take with you." Barbara gave Kira an encouraging smile.

"Thanks."

With breakfast out of the way, Kira called Jared into the living room to work on some deep joint compressions to prepare him for the beach. She took out Jared's therapy mat, laid it out on the floor, and then helped Jared get settled on his back. Next she pushed to compress his ankle and knee joints. Bending his legs, she repeated the process on his hips. He sat up and she continued with his arms and shoulders, all the time describing the feeling of wet sand and cold water to him.

With sensory therapy completed, Jared seemed more able to make eye contact with Kira. He did not offer any hugs, but she was content with the sincere smile he gave her before he headed off to brush his teeth. She hoped the electric toothbrush's vibration would provide more sensory input. The vibrations sometimes helped bring his sensory system into place and helped him focus, especially after sleepless nights or situations that disrupted his routine. If his sensory system was not in order, he might shut down if he became overstimulated on the beach.

Finally ready, they began their adventure. Snacks, blanket, and towels in hand, Kira followed as Jared skipped ahead. For the moment, he seemed happy to be going, although he struggled to keep his footing in the soft sand. She took a quick look for any locals or tourists who might be out walking their dogs. Thankfully, the beach appeared empty this morning.

Jared turned and signed, "Is the water cold?" But before she could answer, he ran toward the water. Kira hurried after him. Studying his face, she could see the combination of amazement and trepidation. He was ready to play in the waves, yet he didn't want them to touch him. "Jared, don't go in above your knees," Kira yelled.

* * *

Watching from the construction site, Grant was perplexed. The boy couldn't be deaf because she talked to him even while he wasn't looking at her. Yet he was clearly signing to her. What could be going on?

"Hey, bro." Brandon slapped him on the shoulder. "Checking out the women? Not too many out there today."

"No," Grant replied. He pointed at Kira. "That's Kira Nichols and her son. She's the one we talked about at dinner last night. Any idea why the boy is signing?"

"Ask Barbara."

"Barbara?"

Brandon rolled his eyes. "Are you aware of *anything* that goes on around here? Barbara is Kira's housekeeper. Before that, she worked for Kira's grandfather. Mom has known her for years. She mentioned all that at dinner last night."

"Well, maybe I'll just go find out for myself." Turning away, Grant headed toward the path and slowly made his way down to the beach.

As Grant approached, Jared continued to run toward the waves and then leap away before the water touched him. Suddenly the boy stopped at the end of the sand and signed furiously at his mother.

"Look at me, Jared," she told him. She signed to the boy as she talked. "I know it hurts. You need to go wash off in the water."

Grant watched as Jared refused to look at Kira. The little boy stood there rocking back and forth. Grant could see that Kira was struggling to stay calm.

She said, "Jared, listen to me. I can't take you back to the house until we deal with this. Go wash your feet off in the water."

Jared shook his head, closed his eyes, and continued rocking.

"Is there anything I can do to help?" Grant asked.

Kira's back stiffened. "Mr. Rutledge, I'm sure you mean well, but do you always just show up and interfere in other people's personal issues?"

"Kira, I saw your son signing and—" He lowered his voice and started again. "I don't mean to interfere. I just . . . it's just that you're alone out here and I thought maybe you needed some help."

She closed her eyes. "Grant. You can't help. I've been dealing with this by myself for years. I know what to do. Please, just leave us alone."

Jared had stopped rocking. He looked more focused now.

"Jared, this is Mr. Rutledge," Kira said as she signed to him. "Grant, my son, Jared. Jared, go wash your feet in the water."

Grant was relieved to see Jared respond to his mother this time. As the boy turned back to the water, Grant heard Kira inhale a long breath and let it out slowly. "I'm sorry if I overstepped my bounds," he said. "Have a good day, Kira. Nice to see you, Jared." He briefly touched her shoulder, but she simply lowered her eyes and turned away.

* * *

From the public parking lot at the end of the beach, the man with the binoculars focused in on Kira. He watched her speak with the guy from the construction site and frowned. It looked like the guy's eyes were glued on her, taking in her every move. He didn't want to have to report that she was involved with someone. No, he needed more time to see exactly what she was up to.

He flipped the binoculars onto the car seat and drummed his fingers on the steering wheel. He wasn't paid enough to run into problems. He picked up his notebook and jotted down his findings and the time.

He glanced at his watch. He had to leave to meet with his client. He smirked. With any luck, he might be able to milk some real money out of this.

Picking up the binoculars again, he took one more look, satisfied that the construction guy had moved on. He threw the glasses down. Putting the car in drive, he pulled into the flow of traffic, his mind racing on what kind of obstacles this job might have.

Chapter 3

Coming to a stop at the construction site early Friday morning, Grant marveled at the shifting pink and purple hues of the sky. Down on the beach, the incoming waves softly lapped the sand.

Unfolding his tall frame from the driver's seat, he got out of the car and perched on the hood to sit and drink in the beauty. No wonder Kira walked the beach so often. What a perfect way to start the morning, getting rid of any leftover tension from the day before.

A sudden movement from behind the lumber pile caught Grant's eye. Without shifting his weight, he turned his gaze to find Jared's eyes focused on his car. The boy seemed completely unaware that Grant had seen him. Jared's fingers were moving in slow motion, signing with his hands in front of him.

"Jared?"

Startled, Jared looked down at the ground and started to rock his upper body gently.

Grant walked cautiously toward the young boy. "Jared? It's me, Grant. We met on the beach the other day. Would you like to see my car?"

Jared suddenly stopped rocking and walked slowly to the car, giving Grant quick looks from the corner of his eye.

"You must like the color red," said Grant. "It is a bright color. When I was a kid, a red sports car was all I ever dreamed about having."

Yet even as he spoke, he thought, "I'm drowning here. What do I say to him? I don't know how to sign. What is he doing with his fingers?"

Jared walked around the car, holding his right hand near his ear, rubbing his fingers together. He turned, stopped in front of Grant, and signed.

"Jared, I don't know sign language. Can you say it to me?" Grant asked.

"I . . . I want a ride," Jared said. He shot Grant a tentative smile, but the look in his eyes was triumphant.

"Hey, that was great, but I think we should ask your mom first."

A pickup truck rumbled behind them, and Jared moved closer to Grant. Without hesitation, Grant put a protective arm around the boy. Then a second pickup arrived. Sam and Brandon were in one, and Marcus was in the other.

Sam and Brandon parked off to the side. As they approached, Grant could see questions in their eyes. Jared had moved behind Grant, staring into space and humming softly.

"Everyone has arrived, it seems," Marcus proclaimed as he exited his truck. "Let's raise some walls."

"Who's this?" Sam said.

"This is Jared," said Grant. "Jared, these are my brothers, Sam and Brandon, and my dad, Mr.—"

"Call me Marcus. Nice to meet you, Jared."

"I'll be right back," Grant told them. "Everything is ready to get started. I'm going to take Jared home. Another time, I'm going to take him for a ride in my car."

At those words, Jared slipped Grant a shy smile and then led the way toward Kira's house.

As they approached the walkway, Grant pointed to the sky. "Jared, look. My dad used to tell me 'pink sky in the morning, sailors take warning.' Sailors used to watch the sky for changes in colors to let them know when it was going to storm."

"I like colors night sunset," Jared said as he signed.

Grant tried to fill in the missing words. Presumably Jared had signed them. "I like the colors at night at sunset, too."

Jared smiled broadly and then ran the rest of the way to the house. At the door, he burst through, leaving Grant alone outside.

Grant waited for the sound of a greeting to confirm that an adult was home. Not hearing anything, he knocked and took a step inside. "Hello?"

"Mr. Rutledge, so nice of you to bring Jared home," A woman with curly gray hair entered the foyer. She guessed that she was about his mother's age—in her early sixties. She finished wiping her hands on a blue-and-white checked towel and flipped it over her shoulder. "Jared was just telling me he went to see your car. I'm Barbara O'Donnell, Kira's housekeeper. It's been a while, so forgive me for not remembering which one of the boys you are."

"I'm Grant, the oldest. Yes, I'm sorry if he was missed. I enjoyed having him there."

"I don't think Kira would like that, but thank you."

"I'm sorry. Have I done something to offend her?" Grant asked.

Barbara chuckled. "Not that I am aware. Kira is just a very private person; she likes to keep Jared close to home."

"I can understand. He seems like a great kid."

"I'm sure you have work to do. I will make sure Jared doesn't disturb you anymore."

"Actually, I promised I'd take him for a ride sometime. Is Kira home?" He glanced around the living room to the right of the foyer. Framed photographs were scattered on the mantle. Soft shades of blue warmed the room. The sofa was worn, but in good shape. A matching easy chair sat facing the fireplace. Cozy.

"I'm afraid not." Barbara smiled. "Is there something you needed to talk to her about?"

Grant tried to hide his disappointment and flashed a grin instead. "No, just that ride. I'll catch her another time." He turned to leave, wondering why he felt emptiness.

Chapter 4

Saturday morning was always quiet at Kira's house. Today she sat out on the deck with the paper and her coffee, half listening for Jared to finish his breakfast in the kitchen. Then the loud rumble of Grant's sports car broke the silence as he pulled up in front of the property next door. Working on a Saturday? So much for a quiet day around here.

Laying the paper aside, Kira walked to the railing and looked out at the ocean. The soft waves lapped the sand as the tide crawled up the beach. Her mind drifted. The night before, Jared had surprised her by initiating some snuggling and bedtime reading. She smiled as she recalled how pleasant it had been to share some words and physical contact with her son.

"Kira?" Barbara's voice broke into her thoughts. "I will be ready in just a few minutes to take Jared to the library."

"Okay. Is he almost ready?"

"I thought he was with you."

"What? I thought he was with you." Kira rushed past Barbara and sped down the hallway toward Jared's room. "Where could he have gone? He never takes off!"

"Maybe he heard Grant's car and walked over there again."

"Again? Are you telling me he's done it before?"

"Just yesterday. Snuck out while I was in the kitchen. Grant brought him back."

"I'll go see." Kira was already halfway out the door.

As she ran down the walkway, Kira saw movement among the newly erected walls at the construction site. She heard Grant's laughter and stopped short. Jared and Grant were sitting on the floor in the sawdust, with Jared's signing book open between them. Jared's fingers were moving slowly; he was teaching Grant a sign. Both of them were oblivious to her appearance.

"Jared? How long have you been here?" Kira said softly. "Barbara and I have been worried about you."

Grant raised his head. "I thought you knew where he was."

"No, I didn't."

Jared grabbed his signing book. He signed to Kira, "Is it time to go with Barbara?"

"Yes, it is," Kira signed back while talking to him. "You are to never leave the house without telling me, Jared. It's not safe."

"I'm sorry, Mom," Jared signed.

Kira kneeled in front of him and hugged him close. "I just don't want anything to happen to you." She kissed him on the forehead. "Go find Barbara and have fun today. Don't eat too many doughnuts!"

"Bye, Grant." Jared smiled, waved, and ran off. Kira's eyes welled at the thought of just how far Jared was progressing. He had been full of surprises lately.

"I'm sorry, Kira. I honestly thought you knew where he was or I would have brought him right back."

"It's okay." Kira sighed. "It's not your problem, Grant. He's a lot to handle at times."

"How about a walk on the beach to help clear some tension?" Grant asked.

Longing for an adult conversation, she hesitated but for a brief moment. "Give me five minutes to make sure Jared is off, and I'll meet you down there."

After making sure Jared and Barbara were off for their Saturday adventure, Kira started down the path to the beach. Grant was already standing near the water with his back to her. She thought, "He's handsome, that's for sure, but keep your wits about you. Your primary focus is Jared. He is the one who needs you the most."

She took a deep breath and approached him. "Hey. It's beautiful, isn't it?"

"Incredible," said Grant. "I never realized how relaxing it could be."

They walked down the beach in silence. She wondered if she had been too outspoken at their first meeting.

"Jared is a very special child," Grant spoke quietly.

"Yes, he is. He has come a long way in the past few years." Kira stopped and looked out at the ocean. Her hazel eyes pooled with tears as she reflected on the progress Jared had made. She blinked rapidly and steeled her emotions.

"Tell me about him."

"Jared was born with autism. We didn't know it at the time. All we knew was that he cried a lot. It was unbearable at times. He couldn't stand to be touched, so it was difficult to console him . . ."

Glancing at Grant, Kira continued her insight of Jared's early years. "Jared was pretty silent except for the crying. There was no cooing or babbling. He didn't make eye contact. When he was about thirteen months old, I called Early Intervention and had him evaluated. He had, at that point, the verbal skills of a three-month-old. I honestly thought he was deaf.

"Early Intervention set him up with a speech therapist, and that's how we started with sign language. The therapist reminded us how frustrating it feels not to be able to communicate, and she was right. Once Jared started learning sign language, some of his aggression disappeared. Things settled down some. Look at him now; he's starting to talk, becoming more verbal. Just last night he wanted to snuggle and read bedtime stories, which is not part of his usual bedtime routine. That is such a huge victory for him."

She closed her eyes and struggled to maintain her composure in front of Grant. She felt him move away from her and was thankful for the space to gather her wits. Jared's autism made her so emotional, yet she needed to keep her heart well protected.

"You're a strong woman, Kira," Grant said softly.

"Grant . . ." She whispered so he wouldn't hear the tears in her voice. "I probably should be getting back."

"No, don't go yet. What about your husband? I don't mean to pry, but my parents mentioned it briefly. Jared couldn't have been very old when your husband died."

Kira cringed at the change of subject. Talking about autism was one thing, her former husband another. She wondered how she could move the conversation elsewhere without appearing rude.

Grant seemed to sense her reluctance. "Like I said, I don't want to pry. I just want to get to know you." He sounded sincere.

"Patrick died when Jared was six months old. Jared doesn't remember him at all."

"What happened—if you don't mind my asking?"

"He was involved in a car accident. I really need to head back now."

They walked in silence all the way back to her house.

When they reached her mailbox, she said, "Thank you, Grant, for the walk. It was relaxing. Just what I needed."

"I hope I didn't push too much. I think you are a very strong woman, Kira, with all that you have been through. When was the last time you had some time to yourself?"

She smiled at his serious expression. "I just did."

"That doesn't count. This is practically still your backyard, and I grilled you with questions the whole time. How about dinner some night?"

"That sounds nice. Maybe soon." Kira tried to remain uncommitted. "Thanks again, Grant." With a quick wave, she ran up the front stairs to her house and moved inside.

* * *

The man with the binoculars leaned back against the car as he watched Kira say goodbye to Grant. Crossing his arms in front of him, he thought back to his latest meeting with the client. Basically, she wanted him to do a bit more digging to ensure that there were no obstacles to her plan. He had made some queries and was waiting for answers. His mind drifted to the football game he was missing. He didn't have a choice with this client. Whatever her motives, she wanted this wrapped up as soon as humanly possible—and maybe even sooner than that. There was no personal time on the clock with this job.

Chapter 5

After a hot shower, Kira curled up in front of the fireplace with a steaming cup of coffee. She replayed the day in her mind. The walk on the beach had relaxed her—for a time. Grant's company had been warm and friendly, inviting Kira to open up, which she had not done in years. But she regretted losing her composure in front of him. It seemed like his incredible blue eyes had dissolved her vow to keep Jared her sole focus.

In fact, those eyes had brought a desire Kira had thought was long past, one that she hadn't felt with Patrick. Ever.

She came out of her daydreams as she heard a car door shut, signaling that Jared and Barbara were home from their daylong excursion. Jared burst through the door, beaming from ear to ear. As he flopped down in front of the fireplace, Kira realized with a bit of disappointment that the quiet was gone. She sipped her coffee and cringed that it had grown cold. Just how much time had passed? Kira shook herself into the present. "How was it?"

"Good," said Jared as he stared at the flames.

"Look at me, Jared, while we talk."

"After the library, we went to visit Marcus and his wife. Barbara knows them. I got to have cookies." Suddenly Jared leaped up and fled the room, his moment of sharing over.

Kira smiled up at Barbara. "At least the verbal is coming in short spurts. So, who is Marcus?"

"Marcus and Mary Lou Rutledge. Mary Lou and I have been friends for years, but we just haven't had time to get together. Jared and I stopped by for a little while after running errands."

"Rutledge? Any relation to next door?"

"Yes, Grant's parents." Barbara headed for the kitchen, calling back, "How was the walk on the beach? I'm assuming you weren't alone."

"Why would you assume that? Don't I always go alone?"

Barbara poked her head back in the living room. A sly grin graced her pretty face. "Were you?"

"Well, not exactly." Kira stood up and paced the floor. "I don't get him. At first he seemed like an egotistical jerk with that fast sports car, and then on the beach, he, well, he just wasn't."

"Just wasn't? More to it than that, I'm sure. So what gives?"

"He asked about Jared. We talked about the autism and the gains Jared's made. It was good to just talk. He's sensitive."

"You mean he's not like Patrick?"

"I wasn't comparing them."

"Maybe not consciously, but I think on some level you were. It's been four years. Not every man is Patrick. Many men are better than him. Just look at the way Grant interacts with Jared; you can see already he's better with children than Patrick would ever have been."

Kira moved uneasily around the room. "I don't like talking about Patrick this way. It wasn't his fault that he couldn't handle Jared's crying."

"No, but it was his fault that he chose to leave you alone that night with the baby. It was his choice to drive so fast. That car accident was his fault, Kira, so stop making excuses for him. It's time to let go. Start living your life again. Let go of the past and the guilt that you're carrying around."

Barbara gently put her hand on Kira's arm. "I know, honey, you might get mad at me. But I'm speaking out of love. I have seen you pour your heart and soul into raising this child. It's time to take care of your heart, too."

"My heart is just fine, Barb."

"Of course it is." Barb removed her hand and headed toward the hallway. Then she called back, "You have it very well barricaded."

Kira shook her head. Maybe her heart *was* barricaded, but with good reason. Even Grant's sports car scared her. What if he was really just another Patrick in disguise?

She walked down the hall to Jared's room. She knocked softly on the door. Jared lay on the floor. He'd lined his Matchbox cars up, making sure they were exactly straight. As she watched him, she wondered if it would be too much to take him out for pizza, considering he'd already had quite a bit of excitement today.

Oh, what the heck. "Jared? How about going for a pizza tonight? Or are you 'out of whack'?" Kira asked.

"I'm okay. I just like to see the cars lined up. Can we get cheese pizza?"

"You bet. Get ready and we'll go in five minutes." Kira headed down the hall. "Barb, we're going for a pizza; you want to come?"

"You two go ahead. I'm have a date with a hot bath and a good book."

As they drove into town, Kira and Jared talked about his day. He told her about Marcus and Mary Lou's house, the warm cookies, and how much he liked Marcus. "He's a lot like Grant. I like Grant," announced Jared.

"He sounds nice," said Kira.

The pizza parlor was quiet for a Saturday night, perhaps because it was still early. They made their way to a table in the back, where Kira knew it would stay relatively quiet for Jared, even if the place suddenly got busy. After she ordered their pizza and sodas, they played tic-tac-toe on the paper placemats while they waited.

"Well, this must be the popular Saturday night dinner." A deep voice came from beside them.

"Grant!" Jared jumped out of his seat to give him a hug.

"Hi, Jared. Kira."

"Hi, Grant." Kira felt her cheeks flush.

"Mom, can Grant have pizza with us?"

"Jared, I'm sure this is a time . . ."

Kira glanced around and saw he was alone. "It's fine. You're welcome to join us. Jared really enjoys your company."

As Grant slid into the seat next to Jared, he said with a sly grin, "Just Jared?"

Now her cheeks felt like they were burning. "I enjoyed your company today, also."

"I saw Marcus," Jared said suddenly.

"You did?" Grant asked.

Kira laughed at his surprise. "Apparently Barb took Jared to see your mom and dad today, and Jared got a taste of your mom's homemade cookies."

"My favorite. Wish I had known she was making cookies. I would have gone with you!"

"You can come to my play at school next week. We are having cookies there."

"Jared. I'm sure Grant has to work. It's in the afternoon, remember." She hoped the pizza would come before she got herself into a mess. How could she get through dinner sitting across from him? He was so good to Jared. Clearly her son just adored him. But would he use Jared to get close to her? Surely not. Barbara knew the family. And then there were those blue eyes . . .

"Kira?"

She was startled out of her daydream. "What?"

"If you wouldn't mind, I would love to go to his play. One of the nice things about my job is that my schedule can be flexible—at least, to a degree. But I don't want to overstep." Grant's eyes locked onto hers. It seemed like he was almost daring her to say yes.

"Please, Mom. I really want Grant to come." Jared's fingers signed with the verbal plea.

"Of course. If Jared would like you there."

Jared went back to drawing on the placement. As he hunched over the picture, his elbow bumped against his soda glass, tipping it over. Though Kira piled napkins on the spill as quickly as she could, it wasn't fast enough to stop the soda from running off the table onto Jared's lap. The rocking started as Jared retreated from their world in a heartbeat.

"I need to get him out of here, and the pizza is on its way now." Kira gestured to the waitress, who was bringing the pizza from the kitchen. "Can you have her put it in a to-go box for me?"

"You get the box, Kira, I'll take Jared to the car. It's okay. I can carry him more easily than you can, and it will be quicker to get him out of the noise. I'll meet you outside." Grant smiled reassuringly at her.

Kira hesitated for a second, not wanting her son out of her sight. Then she realized that the faster she moved, the sooner she'd be with them. She quickly explained the situation to the waitress, who was understanding and headed out back to get a box for the pizza.

As Kira waited, Grant talked quietly to Jared, picked him up firmly, and headed for the door. She waited, holding her breath for Jared to start crying at the strange arms holding him, yet Jared simply settled against Grant's shoulder. With a wink from Grant as they walked by, they went out the door. Kira breathed a sigh of relief.

"You're all set," the waitress said.

Kira thanked her and handed her a twenty-dollar bill.

"Keep the change."

Out in the parking lot, Kira saw Grant leaning against his car with Jared still in his arms.

"I need to get him home. I'm afraid this was too much for him after a day out with Barbara."

"Which car is yours?"

"The blue Honda right there." Kira pointed. "I'm sorry tonight went the way it did."

"I'm not. I got to see you and Jared. This doesn't count as an answer to my dinner invite, though."

She opened the car door and stepped back so Grant could put Jared in his booster seat. Grant buckled him in with ease and kissed him on the forehead. "I'll see you later, buddy."

"'Night," signed Jared.

"Back to signing," stated Grant as he shut the car door.

"Yes, he's back in his world for now. A good night's sleep will do him wonders. He'll be better tomorrow. There are more good days than bad now. He's making a lot of progress."

"Do you want me to follow you home? Will you need help getting him in the house?"

She smiled up at him and said, "No, thank you. I've done this many times before. Besides, you didn't get your pizza."

"I don't care about the pizza, Kira. I just wonder about you and Jared, I mean, well . . ." Grant paused.

"You wonder what?"

"Well, he's quite a heavy boy. I'm sure you know a lot more about that kind of stuff than me. I'm simply saying, he felt like dead weight, and I just wonder how you can lift him when he's like that. You're not exactly a big woman."

"I guess my adrenaline kicks in. And maybe I'm just stronger than I look."

Grant grinned down at her. "Maybe you just are."

Jared started to cry.

"I need to go, Grant. I need to get him home."

As Kira slid into the driver's seat, the crying got louder. Jared started rocking his head from side to side, tugging at his pants. Kira sat there for a moment, unsure of what to do. It was going to be a very long ride home if he cried the whole way. The wet pants were the problem. However, even if she removed his pants and kept him in his undershorts, the sensory feel of the booster seat against his bare skin would disturb him. Either way he was bound to cry. She made a mental note to keep a spare set of clothes in the car.

"Jared, you need to stop. I can't drive with you crying like this." Kira watched him in the rear view mirror. Through his tears, Jared kept signing, "Wet, wet."

"I know it's wet. We can take the pants off, but you might not like the feel of the booster seat. Let's think about what we can do."

Kira got out of the car and went around to unbuckle Jared. For a brief moment at least, he stopped crying. Sighing deeply, Kira felt drained of every ounce of energy.

"You're still here?"

"Grant?"

"I went back in to get a pizza to go. I thought you had left."

"I can't yet. Jared's pants are wet, so he's crying. However, if I take them off he won't be able to stand the feel of the booster seat. I need to find something softer he can sit against so I can take his pants off."

"I have an old chamois shirt in my car. How about wrapping that over the seat?"

She thought, "Why is he being so nice? I could really get used to someone helping me like this."

She nodded her head. "That might work."

Kira started to help Jared remove the wet pants as Grant hurried to his car to get the shirt. She fixed the booster seat and settled Jared once more, reminding him that he'd have the shirt for his legs in a moment. He finally seemed content. The crying was replaced with some singsong humming, a milder type of vibration he did whenever he was distressed.

"Thank you once again," Kira said when Grant returned. "You have been very helpful to me lately."

"I am going to follow you home and help you get him inside. No refusals. You're tired. I can see it. Let me at least just carry him for you tonight."

"Okay. I am tired, and I will admit he's heavy."

"Good. I'll follow you." Grant rubbed her shoulder briefly before he made his way to his car and slipped into the driver's seat.

The drive home was uneventful. Jared continued to hum as Kira listened to soft music on the radio. When she pulled into the driveway, she suddenly realized that Jared was quiet. In fact, he was sound asleep.

Grant met her as she stepped out of the car. "He's out like a light," she told him.

"He should really be dead weight then." Grant smiled. "I'll pick him up, and you can show me to his room."

Leading the way to Jared's room, Kira pulled back the bedcovers for Grant to ease the little boy into bed. She watched Grant's muscles flex as he laid Jared down tenderly so as not to wake him. For a moment, Kira felt her heart melt. This was the first time a man had put her son to bed. Grant gently covered Jared with a blanket and kissed him on the forehead.

Kira leaned over and kissed her son, too. "I love you, Jared."

Then she led Grant back to the living room and collapsed onto the couch. "Barb's out visiting a friend," she explained.

She took a deep breath and said, "I really have to thank you, Grant. I appreciate that you took the time to do that for me."

"It was no problem." Grant sprawled into the easy chair.

"Pizza? I think I left in it the car, but we can reheat it."

"I picked one up, too. Your cheese, or my pepperoni?"

"How about both? I'll get some plates."

By the time Grant returned with the pizzas, Kira had pulled out plates and poured drinks. She put the pizzas in the oven to reheat, and then they returned to the living room.

Kira relaxed for the second time that day in Grant's company, comfortable with the light conversation and intermittent silence. She felt her face soften as they laughed together.

When the oven timer buzzed, she returned to the kitchen, put the pizza on plates, and carried them back to the living room. "It's been a relaxing day overall," she said. "Well, except for the pizza parlor." She grinned at Grant and motioned at the plates, which she set on the coffee table. "So, does this count as dinner for us?"

"Well, I had in mind something a little more romantic than takeout pizza in your living room after a crisis with Jared. Is this as good as I'm going to get?"

"Possibly. Or maybe we can arrange something without a crisis involved." She was surprised at how easy it was to laugh with him.

When they were done eating, Grant picked up the plates and took them to the kitchen. Kira followed him. "Hey, I'll get that."

"I got it."

As she leaned against the counter, Kira admired the way he moved easily around the kitchen, putting the plates in the sink and throwing the trash out. "And the man cleans, too," she thought. "He's just full of surprises."

"What are you smiling at?"

"You. A man who actually knows his way around the kitchen. Now that's a nice surprise."

He moved close to her and looked down into her eyes as he lowered his head to meet hers. He pulled her close to him as his lips teased hers. Kira sighed as Grant gently ended the kiss. Her heart was racing.

"I'll call you tomorrow." Grant brushed her lips tenderly again and then quietly let himself out.

Chapter 6

The sun shining in the window woke Kira on Sunday morning. Her first thoughts were of Jared and his reaction the night before. Then she considered how Grant had taken charge and followed her home. He'd been so sweet. His thoughtfulness had made Jared's episode fade into the background.

Sighing deeply, Kira rose and headed to the shower. The hot water rained over her as she mulled over the side of Grant she had witnessed last night. He seemed to know exactly how to handle Jared. The best part of all was the positive way that Jared had responded. He'd never acted that way with a stranger before.

As she pulled on her favorite jeans and a sweatshirt, she realized that Jared and Barbara were still in bed. Kira tiptoed around, brewing herself a cup of hot, steaming coffee. She stood by the coffeemaker as it gurgled and spit, then made her way to her favorite spot on the deck to watch the ocean. Besides the beach itself, this was the best place to really do some thinking, and thinking was something she needed to do. With a clear head, she could think rationally without stars in her eyes like a lovestruck teenager. Kissing him may have felt like heaven, but this was real life and Jared her first priority.

The ringing telephone jarred Kira from her reflections. "Hello?"

"Good morning." At the sound of Grant's deep voice, her pulse began to race. "I hope I'm not waking you."

"I was up. Enjoying coffee, watching the ocean."

"Did you sleep well?"

"Yes, and you?" Where was this small talk going? Did he want to see her? Did she want to see him?

"I slept well. How's Jared this morning?"

Kira smiled and relaxed. "He's still sleeping."

"I enjoyed last night," Grant said quietly.

Startled by the shift in conversation, Kira paused a moment. Then she said, "I did, too."

"How about some kite flying with Jared today? It's windy enough."

"That sounds good."

"Great. I'll be over in a little while, and I'll bring the kite. And, Kira . . . relax."

"See you then, Grant."

As she walked into the kitchen for another cup of coffee, she pondered Grant's parting remark. Did she really just need to just relax? Was it as simple as that?

Jared bounded into the kitchen, interrupting the silence. "Good morning, Mom."

"Good morning, Jared."

While Jared helped Kira fill the cereal bowls and butter the toast, they talked about what needed to be done for therapy that morning. Then Kira said, "I have a surprise for you later today."

"What is it?" Jared signed.

"No. Use your voice," Kira said.

"What is it?" he said.

"How would you like to fly a kite later today?"

"Yeah!"

Kira smiled. "Okay. First, you have to clean up those cars on the floor in your room. Then when Grant gets here—"

"Grant's coming?"

"Yes, he's going to fly the kite with us."

"Can I pick up the cars now?" Jared asked.

"Finish breakfast first. Don't forget your juice."

Kira cleaned up the breakfast dishes while Jared hurriedly straightened his room. Then he kept watch at the open window until he heard the rumble of Grant's car. With a huge grin, he was outside the door before Grant could exit the car. Kira could hear them out in the driveway.

"Hi, Grant!"

"Hi, Jared. Ready to fly a kite?"

"Yeah! Mom, can we go now?" Jared flew into the house and wrapped his arms around her legs. Kira handed him his sweatshirt.

"Go ahead down with Grant. I'll let Barb know where we will be." She looked at Grant, who was standing in the doorway. "If that's all right with you?"

"That's fine. We'll meet you down there." Grant's voice warmed her once again.

A few moments later, she followed them down to the beach. As she watched from a distance, Grant helped Jared set up the kite and attach the string to it. Soon they had it flying in the wind.

"I'm doing it myself!" Jared yelled to Grant, who stood off to the side.

"Great job!" Grant looked over his shoulder and quickly smiled at Kira before returning his attention back to the boy. "Let out on the string a little bit, Jared."

Kira continued to walk slowly toward them, watching the interaction between them. Jared's face glowed as he flew the kite, with Grant calling out instructions every so often. She pulled out her camera and took a few pictures.

"Thank you. This was a great idea," Kira said, finally coming up behind Grant.

"You're welcome. I'm glad you were both able to join me."

"Grant!" Jared yelled as the kite took a nosedive into the sand. Grant ran to help the boy get the kite back up into the wind. As they worked together, Kira snapped more pictures.

An hour or so later, with the kite-flying adventure behind them, Jared went to his room for some quiet time. Kira and Grant sat in the living room, enjoying the warmth out of the wind. Kira relished the fact that Jared's autism seemed almost unnoticeable today. With the distraction of the kite, he'd handled the beach just fine.

After a while, Grant broke the silence. "One of the small inns in town has a restaurant with great food. How about some lunch?"

"I'm not so sure how Jared would do after such a busy morning," Kira said. "Remember, he was busy yesterday, too."

Barbara entered the room. "I hope I'm not interrupting, but I wanted to say hello."

"Hi, Barbara. We're just talking about lunch," said Grant.

"Oh, great idea," Barbara said. She looked at Kira with a mischievous smile. "Why don't you two go ahead. Jared and I will get to spend some time together."

"Barb, you don't need to sit with him," Kira protested.

"Bah! It's my pleasure. You know he's the closest I'll have to a grandson. So, go on, you two. Off with you, it's my afternoon with Jared."

Kira thought she actually saw Barbara wink at Grant.

"Sounds great," he said.

"Okay, Barb. If you don't mind." Kira felt a bit cornered. "Let me go change real quick."

Kira stood in front of her closet and chewed her bottom lip. She didn't want to overdress. Grant was in jeans and a long-sleeved polo shirt. She finally pulled out a pair of black jeans to replace the worn pair she had on, and a lavender short-sleeve sweater. Standing in front of her mirror, she looked one way and then the other. Maybe a different color sweater . . . or different pants. No, it would have to do. She grabbed her brush and pulled her hair up with a clip, then let it fall down again.

She brushed her eyelashes with mascara. Finishing, she stared at herself in the mirror. She took a deep breath and went out to start the first date she'd had in more than four years.

* * *

Kira's stomach tightened as she settled into Grant's MG. She hadn't been in a fast car since Patrick's. She took a deep breath to try to calm herself as she buckled the seatbelt.

"All set?" asked Grant.

"Yes," she answered, praying her voice sounded steady.

Grant started into town at a reasonable speed. At the first stop sign, he briefly reached over for Kira's hand and gave it a reassuring squeeze—as if he knew she was anxious to be in his car. Then realizing she had been holding her breath, she let it out with a sigh.

"How long have you had this car?" Kira asked.

"Quite a while now. It took a long time to fix her up. It's been a work in progress. A long time coming."

Kira noted the pride in his voice. "You restored it yourself?"

"Yeah. It's a hobby."

Grant turned on a channel with soft classical music, and they rode in silence the rest of the way to town. Kira wondered what Grant really was all about. He certainly had shown her a thoughtful, gentle side.

Grant pulled into the parking lot behind the small inn. "Here's the restaurant I was telling you about. It used to be just a bed and breakfast, but the owners turned the porch into a small dining room that's open to the public. My dad helped work on the job."

Grant held open the door as Kira entered a small foyer. The lights were low, but not too dark. She could see that the porch had been expanded, and now high-backed booths offered privacy to all the patrons. Paintings of ocean scenes filled the walls, and the Waverly curtains gave the room the cozy feeling of home.

Kira watched Grant check out the other diners. "See anyone you know?"

"No. Old habits die hard, I guess." Grant laughed. "My brothers and I used to people watch when we came here with our parents for brunch."

The hostess led them to a quiet booth in the back, and Kira slid into the seat across from Grant.

"Tell me about your childhood," Kira said.

"I grew up right here in town with my two younger brothers. Mom is a great cook, which Jared can already attest to with the cookies." Grant smiled at Kira. "My dad and I spent a lot of time together doing projects. When I was about Jared's age, maybe a little older, we worked together on a tree house. Dad did most of it, but he sure made me feel important by letting me help. I remember that clear as anything."

"It sounds like you're very close to your mom and dad."

"Yes, we're a pretty close family."

"Sounds nice. Where did you go to college?"

"I went to a small business college in Texas. It was fun, but I missed the ocean. I had forgotten just how relaxing it was to be near it."

"I know what you mean. I spend every morning having my coffee watching the waves and the tide. I'm fascinated by tides—how they work, why they work. I couldn't imagine starting the day any other way."

"I stayed down south for a while. I worked a bunch of construction jobs to see how other companies set things up. Just came back about a year ago when my dad talked about semi-retiring. Decided it was time to come back and help with the family business."

Grant and Kira sat in thoughtful silence.

"Are you glad you're back involved in the family business?" Kira asked. "Or was that more of an obligatory matter?"

Grant smiled. "I'm definitely glad to be back. I don't feel obligated to my dad at all. Besides, he wouldn't have it that way in the least. He was all for my brothers and me going off and doing what would have made us the happiest. I love following in Dad's footsteps. He was the best teacher I have ever had."

They ordered, and when they sat back to wait for the food, Grant gave Kira his full attention. "Tell me more about autism. You must be an expert on the subject."

"I don't know if I am an expert, but I certainly have become very familiar with some of the elements. Every autistic child is different. That is the reason it is difficult to diagnose." She took a deep breath. "A lot of controversy surrounds autism and where it comes from, but certainly in Jared's case, it is something he was born with. A neurologic disorder that affects his sensory system, and in his case, his verbal skills. Not every child has the same symptoms, and it can affect sensory more than verbal, or vice versa. In Jared's case, he was completely nonverbal. Like I told you the other day, the crying was nonstop, but nothing else."

"Will he outgrow it?" Grant leaned forward and rested his arms on the table.

"Children don't necessarily outgrow autism, but they certainly learn to cope better as they get older, so the symptoms seem to lessen."

The waitress returned with their lobster rolls. "They have the best fries here," Grant said.

Kira bit into one and smiled. "You're right." Then she tried the roll. "The lobster is delicious, too."

As they finished their lunch, she directed the conversation back to Grant's childhood. His affection for his dad was obvious.

The waitress reappeared. "Dessert?"

"Just coffee for me," Kira said.

"Me too." Grant sat back. "I have been talking quite a bit. What about your childhood? Was it a happy one?"

Kira played with her spoon, trying to form the words. The waitress came with the coffee, and she released the breath she was holding, relieved for the distraction. She decided to avoid the question.

"Tell me about the house that's going up." Kira sipped her coffee, hoping the change of subject would go smoothly.

"Well, it's being built as a spec house, but there's always the option of myself buying it to settle down. It's all up in the air at the moment."

She wasn't sure if Grant had noticed that she had avoided his question, but she was relieved when he continued to talk about the house and the joy he felt while building.

She was quite relaxed on the ride home, and they rode in comfortable silence. Once again, the classical music played softly in the background.

Grant pulled into the driveway. As he shut the car off, Kira turned to look at him. His eyes met hers and locked for a brief moment before Kira shyly looked away. She said, "I had a great time today, Grant. It really was fun."

"It was. We should do it again sometime."

"Jared's play is this week, Tuesday at one. But please don't feel you have to go."

"I wouldn't miss it." Grant brushed his fingers slowly across her jaw line, turning her head to his. "Kira, look at me."

Kira looked up into his blue eyes, her heart racing. Grant slowly lowered his lips to cover her trembling ones. As his lips caressed hers, she felt herself begin to respond. Then she pulled back from him slowly.

"I should be getting in. I need to check on Jared," Kira said. She could hear that her voice was shaking.

"Kira, wait."

"Grant. Please. I'll see you at the play on Tuesday. It's at the preschool on Foster Road." She closed the car door softly behind her and moved toward the house.

Chapter 7

The preschool's rec room was crowded with parents and grandparents. Kira and Barbara had arrived early to get good seats so Jared would be able to make eye contact with Kira throughout the short program.

"Is Grant coming?" Barbara asked.

"He said he was, though I told him he didn't have to." Kira looked around.

"He will probably show then. We'll save a seat for him." She moved her purse to an empty chair.

"What exactly are you hoping is going to happen here, Barb?" Kira tried to look stern for a moment but then she simply smiled.

"Not a thing. All I would say is listen to your heart, not your head. Isn't that Jared's teacher trying to get your attention?"

"Yes. I'll be back. Hopefully he is okay." Kira made her way to the tall redhead standing in the doorway.

"Hi, Ms. Cheryl. How's Jared doing?"

"Not so well. Right now he's sitting in a corner. Do you think you could help us get him into his place in line? We're almost ready to start."

"Of course. He's probably a bit overwhelmed. He may need a little sensory therapy before you get started. Let me talk to him."

"Thank you so much. He's done well so far this year. I hope giving him a speaking part wasn't too much. It's only one line."

Kira followed Ms. Cheryl down the hall to the room where the class was waiting. Jared was sitting in the corner, just watching the other kids. To Kira, he didn't appear overwhelmed to the point of not being able to participate—just distracted. She knelt beside him. "Jared, are you okay?"

"Hi, Mom," Jared signed.

"Need therapy?" Kira signed.

"Yes."

Kira talked quietly to Jared and cued him on how the preschool program would go as they went through a set of deep joint compressions to help him focus once again. She reminded him that the rec room would be crowded and could be quite loud, but she also explained that it should be quiet during the program while the kids performed. After the sensory therapy was complete, Jared looked Kira directly in the eyes.

"Thank you, Mom." He gave Kira a hug. "I'm okay now."

"Good. Remember you just have to tell Ms. Cheryl when you need therapy. Don't shut down. You have to tell her."

"Okay. I will."

"I'm going to sit in the audience with Barbara. I will see you after the program."

"Is Grant here?"

"He might be by now. He said he'd be here, so I am sure he will. I love you, Jared. You will do fine. Remember your line."

"Okay, Mom."

From the doorway of the rec room, Kira spotted Grant motioning to her. She breathed a sigh of relief. At least he hadn't let Jared down.

"Is Jared okay?" Grant asked when Kira moved Barb's purse to the floor and sat down.

"Yes, he's fine now. He needed some sensory therapy, but he's all set."

"Good. I was worried when Barbara said they needed help with him." Grant reached for her hand.

Giving his fingers a reassuring squeeze, she said, "Thanks."

The kids performed a series of fairy tales, and Jared was one of the three little pigs. When he said, "My house is made of straw!" her heart swelled with pride. It didn't seem possible that he could perform in front of a crowd like this. Tears filled her eyes as he spoke his line.

"Other parents take their kids' small victories for granted," Kira thought, "but Jared has come so far. We're so blessed."

"He did good," Grant whispered.

Kira nodded. "Yes. Who would've thought even a year ago that this could be possible?"

The room turned into utter chaos as the program ended. Kids scattered to find their families and guests to bring them to get refreshments. Jared, beaming from ear to ear, was extremely excited to see Grant.

"You're here!" Jared slapped a high-five to Grant.

"I wouldn't have missed it. You did great, Jared," Grant said. "Now where are those cookies you promised me?"

"Can we get some now, Mom?" Jared asked.

"Absolutely. How about Barb?"

"Count me in," Barb said. "I happen to know who brings them every year, and I wouldn't miss them!"

Jared took Grant by the hand and led the way to the refreshment table. As she walked with Barbara behind them, Kira could see Jared talking along the way, showing Grant things he had made in class.

"I've never seen Jared open up to anyone else before," she said to Barbara. "How did that happen?"

Barbara smiled. "Grant's a nice man, Kira. And your little boy is growing up!"

At the refreshment table, Kira was in for another surprise. The woman handing out cookies seemed to know Grant, Jared, and Barbara. It took Kira a moment to place her.

"Hi, Mary Lou," Jared said.

Kira could see that Grant hadn't expected this.

"Mom? What are you doing here?"

"I have been making cookies for the preschool program since you and your brothers were here. Just something I never stopped doing. Keeps me young and involved."

"Jared asked me to come to his program," Grant said.

"We're having cookies together," Jared volunteered.

"Well, then help yourself. Get a napkin," Mary Lou said. "Hello, Barbara. Kira, it's been quite a while since I have seen you."

"Hello, Mrs. Rutledge."

"Please, call me Mary Lou."

"Mary Lou, then. I wanted to thank you for being so kind to Jared when he was at your house with Barb. He enjoyed your cookies immensely. I heard about them for days."

Mary Lou laughed. "That's how it is with boys. Win them through their stomachs."

"Hmm, sounds somehow like an insult." Grant smiled.

"Come on, Jared. You're holding up the line. Nice to see you again, Mary Lou," Kira said.

"You too, Kira. Grant, why don't you three come out for dinner tonight?" Mary Lou said. "I'm roasting a chicken. Sam and Brandon both have other plans, so they'll be plenty. Barbara, you're welcome too,"

"Kira?" Grant asked.

"Sounds wonderful."

"I think I'll pass, Mary Lou," Barbara said. "I seem to enjoy the quietness around the house more and more these days. It will do these young people good to go out, and it will do me good to stay in and have the house to myself. Thanks just the same."

"You're always welcome, Barb, and you know it," Mary Lou said. "But I certainly understand needing some quiet time, too."

"What time should we come over, Mrs. . . . um, Mary Lou?" Kira asked.

"Oh, I can pick you up!" Grant said. "We can move Jared's booster seat into my car. I've promised him a ride."

Kira paused and looked at Barb, her eyes wide with fear.

"That sounds great," Barb said firmly.

"Well, maybe, but . . ." Kira protested.

"Kira, what is it?" Grant asked.

"Grant, why don't you go help your mom bring all those empty containers back out to her car." Barb nudged Grant toward the refreshment table. "We'll bring Jared back to his classroom and join you in a few minutes."

"Okay. Is everything all right?"

"Yes, it's fine. We'll be right back," Kira answered.

After they walked with Jared to Ms. Cheryl's classroom, Barb pulled Kira aside in the hall. "Listen to me. You need to trust me on this one. I know you're nervous about putting Jared in Grant's car. But you rode in it and you were fine. Grant has never done anything to put Jared in harm's way. You have seen the way he acts with Jared. He adores him. Like I said earlier, trust your heart in this, not your head. Kira, you've got to let go and have fun."

"Okay. I know you're right. It's just hard sometimes."

"That's your head talking logic. Listen to your heart."

* * *

Shortly after five, Grant picked them up. Barbara stood in the doorway and waved goodbye. "See you later, Jared," she called. "Have fun."

Kira gripped the boy's hand tightly. "Okay, Jared. Let's go. You get to ride in Grant's car tonight."

"Yay!" Jared ran toward the car door.

Grant put a hand on her shoulder. "Is everything okay now?"

"Yes, everything's good." She forced a smile. "Let's go. Should we be bringing anything?"

"Nope, not a thing. Mom always has everything under control." Grant gave her a quick hug. "Let's go. Jared's been dying for this ride."

Once again, Grant took charge and buckled Jared into his booster seat. Jared was so excited. He talked in half sentences; his fingers were flying. "How fast can we go?" asked Jared.

Before Kira could answer, Grant spoke. "We only go as fast as the speed limit, Jared. Just because this is a sports car, it doesn't mean that we drive really fast."

As Kira sat back and pondered Grant's answer, she wondered if he really felt that way or if his reply was purely for Jared's benefit.

"Penny for your thoughts?" Grant asked.

"Oh, nothing."

As they drove up the driveway to the Rutledge home, Jared grew increasingly excited. "We're here, we're here!"

"Calm down, Jared. You need to remember that you're at someone else's house," Kira cued. "You cannot run or touch anything."

"I know."

"Kira, he's okay," Grant said. "Are you? You seem nervous."

"I'm okay. This is just a nice place. I don't want him to break anything."

"Don't worry about it. This house has withstood three growing boys. And we weren't angels, believe me. He'll be fine." Grant ran his fingers down her jaw line. Staring deep into her eyes, he said, "You're so beautiful."

Kira smiled. "Is your plan to leave Jared strapped in the booster seat the whole time?"

Laughing, Grant got out of the car and unbuckled Jared. "Killjoy."

Jared immediately ran across the lawn, chasing a butterfly.

Kira shook her head and said, "Where does he get all his energy?"

"You don't have the energy to chase butterflies anymore?" Grant said. "I'm disappointed." He wrapped his arms around her and kissed her softly on the lips. "I hope that doesn't tire you out too much."

"Very funny. You're quite the joker." Kira playfully pushed him away. "Where did Jared go?"

"Probably around back. Let's go see." He grabbed her hand and they walked around to the back of the house, where they found Jared staring up into a very large apple tree.

Marcus came around the house from the opposite direction. He approached Jared and said, "Looks like you found the old tree house. Grant used to spend hours up in that old thing. He helped me build that when he just a little bit older than you."

"Cool. Can I go in it?"

"Jared . . ." Kira started.

Grant put a reassuring arm around her. "Let's see what Mom is doing inside."

"But . . ."

"No buts. Dad has it under control. Don't worry. Let the boys bond."

They went in through the back door to find Mary Lou bustling around the kitchen.

"Welcome, you two. Where's Jared?"

"Hi, Mary Lou," Kira said. "Jared and Marcus are out back, discussing an old tree house of Grant's."

"Ah, the tree house. Marcus and Grant spent hours building that thing. Then, Grant wouldn't come out of it.

He spent just about every waking moment in there. It was a great father-son project."

"I'll let you two chat," Grant said. "I'm going to head back out. I haven't spent much time in the tree house, and it'll be fun to get back in it."

"Do you think it's still safe after all these years?" Kira asked Mary Lou.

"If it isn't, Marcus and Grant will have it stable in no time for Jared to play in. Don't fret. Those two will keep their eye on him."

Kira gave a half smile. "You probably think I'm overprotective. On some levels, I probably am. He just has had so many obstacles to overcome. I worry about him. It's hard not to."

"That's part of being a good mother, Kira. Come sit down."

Mary Lou poured them some hot coffee and set out some cookies. "I can't seem to help it. Cookies are just so comforting. Kira, honey, I have no idea what your own childhood was like, but I do know that you and Jared have had a rough start of it. It's okay that you're overprotective. It's natural. Grant tells us what an amazing mom you are. He says that Jared has made a lot of progress in a short of amount of time through therapy and your dedication. Not all mothers put that much time into rearing their children."

"No, I guess not. It hasn't been easy, but I want Jared to have as normal of a life as possible. Barbara has been a lifesaver. Years ago, I would come here in the summer to visit my grandfather, and she was his housekeeper. I honestly don't know what I would have done without her after the accident." Kira took a sip of her coffee.

"Where are your parents? Do you hear from them?"

"My dad died a few years back. I haven't really heard from my mother since I was eighteen. When I was growing up, she was too involved in her real estate career to notice me. I pretty much brought myself up. Dad spent most of his time drinking." Kira reached for a cookie. "I called my mom when Jared was born. She told me she was too young to be a grandmother. That was the end of the conversation. I haven't heard from her since. Barbara is more Jared's grandmother."

"Well, you have every natural instinct to protect Jared. Sounds like you didn't have many good role models." Mary Lou shook her head. "It's a shame. I just can't imagine having a grandson and not acknowledging him."

Mary Lou stood and started the final touches for dinner. As Kira rose to help, she gestured for her to sit back down. "You just sit. I haven't had someone to talk to in the kitchen for a long time. I'm usually outnumbered by men around here. I'm really enjoying your company."

"Are you sure? I feel like I should be helping."

"I'm positive. Next time I'll put you to work, but this time you just sit and talk."

"I'm not sure what else to say. I honestly never talk about my childhood to anyone." She added, "I never wanted to, until now. I feel so comfortable here."

"It's a lot to keep inside. You need to talk it all through. Get it out. It's the only way to heal."

"You sound a lot like Barb. She's always telling me to listen to my heart, and stuff like that."

"Not bad advice, you know."

Just then, Jared bounded into the kitchen, followed closely by Grant and Marcus. "Mom, the tree house is so cool."

"Did you get to go in it?" Kira asked.

"No. Grant says it needs work. But he says that maybe I can come back someday soon, and me and Marcus and Grant can fix it up. All of us. Grant and Marcus first made it together when Grant was little, like me!"

"That sounds like fun," Kira said. "You should wash your hands now for dinner."

"Okay."

"Come on, Jared, I'll show you where," Grant said.

Kira helped Mary Lou finish setting the table. Marcus carved the chicken, and they all sat down to eat.

Most of the dinner conversation centered on the tree house. Jared was almost too excited to eat. After much coaxing, Kira finally managed to have him finish a few bites of chicken and a serving of potatoes.

After dinner, Grant and Marcus washed dishes while Mary Lou took Kira outside to look at her garden. Once again, Jared chased butterflies across the lawn.

When they went back in the house, Kira said, "I think I need to get Jared home, Grant. He's had a pretty full day, and I really want to end it on a positive note."

"Do you think he's getting overloaded?"

"It can happen quickly. I just don't want him to spiral out of control before we get home." Kira turned toward Mary Lou and Marcus. "I hate to eat and run. I hope you understand."

"Absolutely, Kira," said Mary Lou. "He's still young, and with the program at school, it's been a busy day. I'm so glad you came tonight. We've enjoyed having you both." As she gave Kira a hug, she whispered, "I'm here anytime you need to talk."

"Thank you." Kira kissed Mary Lou on the cheek. "Thank you, Marcus. Jared enjoyed it."

"Bye, Marcus. Bye, Mary Lou," Jared said.

The drive home was quiet. Grant kept the volume of the music turned low, and Jared was almost asleep instantaneously. Kira replayed the day's events in her mind. She hadn't shared her childhood with anyone before, and yet Mary Lou had been so easy to talk to. It felt strange, yet it warmed Kira. She suddenly found herself longing for a family lifestyle she had never had.

The instant Grant turned the car into the driveway, Jared awoke and started talking about the tree house again. "It's time to go in and get ready for bed, Jared," Kira said.

"Okay, Mom. But when can we go back and work on the tree house?"

"I don't know. Right now, you need to go in the house and get in your pajamas, and brush your teeth."

"Okay."

Unbuckled and ushered into the house, Jared bounded down the hall to get ready for bed. Kira turned to Grant. "Can you stay for a little bit?"

"I'd like that."

"Want to start a fire, or should we sit on the deck after I get Jared in bed?" Kira asked.

"Let's sit on the deck. It's a little chilly, but I know you love watching the ocean."

"Okay. Give me a few minutes."

Jared, with the covers tucked in snug around him, kissed Kira good night. After a few short songs to send him off to sleep, she shut off the light and returned to the living room.

Leaning against the doorway, she watched Grant. He was looking at photos along the mantel—photos of Jared as a baby and Kira and Jared together over the past couple of years. She admired his profile, the angular jaw shadowed with the day's growth of beard. He leaned closer to study the pictures, gazing at each for a few seconds before moving to the next. She wondered what he was thinking. He picked up a wide silver frame, holding it close for a moment.

Kira knew the frame contained a snapshot of her pushing two-year-old Jared on the swings at the park. Barbara had captured one of those serendipitous moments when Jared was giggling and she was smiling and even the sky seemed magically blue. She loved that picture.

"Ready?" she asked, a bit reluctant to interrupt Grant. She moved out to the deck.

"Yes." Grant put down the last picture and followed her. "Nice pictures of you and Jared. But I'm curious to know why you don't have any of Patrick."

Kira shivered as though a dark cloud had just covered the setting sun. "Why would you ask something like that?" she snapped.

"Just a question. I figured you would have at least one picture of your husband."

"He has been dead for the past four years. Why would I still have pictures of him around? And why on earth are we talking about this?" Kira started pacing. She tried to steady her breathing. She felt like her lungs were being squeezed.

"It was just a question. Why are you so upset?" Grant asked.

"Never mind."

"You have to talk to me, Kira. Why do you shut me out whenever the subject of Patrick comes up? You have this barrier around you. Heaven forbid that you let me in even a little bit. When are you going to trust me?" Grant crossed his arms, his stance rigid as he leaned against the railing.

"Who says I don't trust you?"

"It's written all over you. You didn't want to let Jared in my car today. You didn't want him in the tree house. Do you think I'd let something harm him? Was Patrick that terrible to him?"

"How dare you?" She planted her feet firmly, hands on her hips, and glared at him. "You have no idea how I feel or what I think."

"You're right. I don't know. You won't talk to me." Grant walked closer to her. "I know when I kiss you, you respond. I feel your body tremble. I know you want me as much as I want you." Grant ran his fingers through some loose strands of hair around her cheek, pushing them back behind her ear. "I see your lips part when I move closer to you, and I know you want that kiss as much as I want it."

His hot breath seared her cheek as he talked softly against her. She closed her eyes, willing herself not to respond to him.

Suddenly Grant moved away. "Then you push me away. Shut me out. What is it you want, Kira?"

Kira stared at him. "Don't do this, Grant."

"Don't do what?"

"Don't push."

"Don't push? Kira, I'm not. I want to get to know you. In case you haven't noticed, I like you. And I think you're a terrific mom."

"There are just some things I'm not ready to share." Kira faced the darkening ocean and took a deep breath.

"When, Kira? When Jared is grown and you're alone? When will be the right time to let someone in?" Grant shook his head.

"Let it go, Grant. Please." Kira could hear the ice in her tone as she hardened her heart again. How had she let herself get in this situation? Surely a relationship would only lead to more pain.

"Fine. Suit yourself." With those words, Grant stormed out. The door slammed and Kira heard the squeal of tires as he raced off down the road.

"Oh, God, what have I done? Don't let it happen again," Kira prayed. Her knees buckled. She sank onto the deck, once again lost in pain and grief.

Chapter 8

Back at his parents' house, Grant slammed the door behind him. He paused just inside the door to take a deep breath, hoping to calm the frustration. No such luck. He stormed into the living room, eyes blazing. "Where's Dad?"

"He's gone to the kitchen for a glass of water. He'll be right back." Mary Lou put her knitting aside. "What's got you all fired up?"

"Nothing."

Grant paced the living room until Marcus entered, carrying a tall glass that was clinking with ice cubes.

"Hello, Son. I didn't expect you back here tonight."

"Honestly, neither did I. But I wanted to let you know that I'm heading out in the morning to check out that property up the coast. You know, the one that might work for a subdivision. Sam and Brandon can handle the oceanfront house. The framing is done. Anything they have questions on, they can come to you."

"Last week you said you didn't want to go after that property," Marcus said. "Why now all of a sudden?"

Grant shrugged. "I've been thinking about it, that's all, and I just decided it's a good idea to look at it again. I'll be gone a couple of weeks."

"Well, you sure sling the bull with the best of them," Mary Lou proclaimed as she stood up. "Sounds more like you're running for the door. Must have been one hell of a fight you and Kira had tonight."

"Nothing like that at all."

"Hmmm. Well, you're old enough to find your own way. Have a safe trip, Grant." She stretched and yawned. "Actually, I was just heading up to bed. I need to finish my novel before my book group meets on Friday. Keep in touch."

She gave Grant a hug and kissed his father goodnight. "See you in bed, Marcus."

The men watched Mary Lou leave the room. "Don't even say it, Dad," Grant started. "She's right. I'm old enough to make my own mistakes—if I'm even making one—but right now, I'm headed out of town. I need to put some distance between me and Kira."

"I hope you know what you're doing, son."

"I don't. Apparently. But she has me at arm's length and won't let me get any closer. I need to clear my head, and I can't be near her to do it." Grant continued to pace the living room floor. "I feel this connection to her, but I don't know how to get through to her. She's feisty and makes me feel alive, but she pushes me away at the same time. God help me, I think I'm falling in love with her." He paused and frowned. "I mean, where did that just come from? I hardly even know her."

* * *

Kira awoke the next day feeling like she had sand dunes in her eyes. She squinted at the clock. It was almost seven. It had been a long night. After Grant had stormed out, she had cried for over an hour. Finally, dragging herself into bed, she had cried herself to sleep. Then she woke every couple of hours, convinced there had been another car accident.

She sat up in bed and turned on the local news station. A perky blonde newscaster was listing the economic merits of the upcoming foliage season. No news of any crashes. "Pull yourself together!" she told herself. "He's not Patrick!"

Kira rose and headed to the kitchen. A pot of strong coffee was what she needed to jumpstart her brain.

As she waited for the coffee to brew, she wandered around the living room, looking at the photos on the mantel. She picked up the one from the park. Grant had seemed to like it. Boy, she had really blown it last night. Of course a man from such a happy family would assume that everything had been fine between her and Patrick. Why had she jumped into being defensive instead of just allowing him to get to know her? He had yet to prove himself to be the jerk that she kept expecting him to be.

In the kitchen, she filled a coffee cup and added cream and sugar. Absently stirring it, she wondered what she should do next. She thought, "I have no idea how to apologize for this. I have no idea even how to proceed with this relationship." She stared out the window, sipping her coffee. Then her thoughts shifted the other way. "No. No relationship. I need to just concentrate on Jared. I don't need to get involved with Grant. It was a mistake in the first place."

Kira started down the hall with new determination. Changes needed to be made in this house, in Kira's life. She was ready. She had stumbled, maybe even fallen for a moment, but she was up again—and with a renewed will. She was ready to begin again.

"Jared, wake up. It's time to get ready for school."

"School today?" Jared sat up, blinking as though he wasn't quite sure where he was.

"Yes, school today. Then we're going to stay home for a quiet afternoon and evening. Just you, me, and Barbara." Kira started out of the room and then paused at the door. "Get dressed and come for breakfast."

Kira dropped Jared off at preschool. Then, breathing out a sigh of relief, she squared her shoulders and drove to the local coffee shop.

She had loved this small town as a child, and now that she was a grown woman, her feelings were even stronger. She was especially fond of the quaintness of the main street, which was lined with shops and eating places. Summertime was filled with the happy chaos that tourism brings. The offseason was Kira's favorite, though. Fall was definitely the best. With the change of seasons and the weather cooling, the town became quiet and peaceful.

Now, settled into a quiet corner with a hot coffee and the local paper, she opened to the want ads. It was time to move on.

For four years she had been Jared's mainstay. At his beck and call, handling therapy sessions and learning sign language, studying about autism, doing what she had to do to make sure Jared mainstreamed into the "normal life." Well, it seemed like they had done it. Jared was doing well in preschool. Kira needed to pick herself up and move on with the next phase of her life. And she certainly didn't need a man for that.

As her eyes wandered over the help wanted ads, Kira realized she wasn't sure what she wanted to do. Instead of going to college, she had worked as a waitress for a few years. After that, she hadn't needed to work. Patrick's salary as a chemical engineer was more than enough to support both of them, and then she had received the heartbreaking news that her grandfather had died, leaving her the house in Maine. As a girl she had spent several happy summers there, taking long walks with him on the beach that she still loved so much. In fact, it was during that joyful period that she had first met Barbara, her grandfather's part-time housekeeper.

She paused and fought back tears, remembering what had happened next. Her mother, difficult at the best of times, had argued bitterly with her grandfather when Kira was about thirteen. She had refused to allow Kira to ever speak to him again. By the time Kira was eighteen, she and her grandfather had completely lost touch.

"Kira?"

Kira looked up and saw Grant's mom.

"Hi, Mary Lou." She smiled. "What a nice surprise."

"I was out doing some errands and thought a cup of hot tea would hit the spot. I was going to get it to go, but would you mind if I joined you instead?"

"Not at all." Kira moved her paper, hoping Mary Lou hadn't noticed the want ads.

"What have you been up to while Jared is at school?"

"I'm just enjoying some quiet time."

Mary Lou nodded encouragingly. "You need that. Looking for a new job? What is it you do now?"

"Oh, well, I . . . um, I was just looking," Kira stammered.

"I hope I'm not intruding," Mary Lou said. She seemed surprised by Kira's response.

"No, not at all. It's just, well, I don't really work right now. When Patrick died, the insurance policy was enough to cover our expenses. I didn't have to work, and I wanted to just concentrate on Jared. But lately things have been going so well with him, I've been thinking of looking for something part-time to keep me busy while he's in school. I'm just not sure what to do. I don't have a lot of experience."

"I see. There's no shame in that. It's quite admirable you have been able to take care of Jared this way. I think it's great that you're looking. What are you interested in?"

"I'm not sure, honestly," Kira said. Then she laughed and gestured at the want ads. "This is all new to me."

"Well, let's see what is out there." Mary Lou reached for the paper.

They perused the paper, laughing as Mary Lou read some of the ads aloud. "Cleaning dental instruments? Maybe not. Night watchman? Ditto."

Kira checked her watch and realized the time had flown by. "I have to pick up Jared."

"Go on. If I hear of anything, I'll give you a call." Mary Lou gave her a hug.

"Please don't mention this to anyone. I'd rather not say anything until I decide what I'm going to do."

"Your secret is safe with me. Don't worry."

Kira gave Mary Lou a kiss on the cheek and hurried to pick up Jared. She realized that Mary Lou hadn't said a word about Grant. Despite her earlier resolve, disappointment coursed through her as she realized she had no idea if she would hear from him again.

* * *

Today the man's binoculars sat idle in his backpack. She hadn't noticed him in the coffee shop, so he had been able to sit quite close. From what he had overheard, it seemed like she was looking for a job. A motherly woman had stopped by the table to help her, but he hadn't been able to catch her name. Now that they were both gone, he jotted his observations in his small notebook. There didn't seem to be much in the way of new developments. Yes, he had to agree with his client: She looked like an easy target. He was still waiting on background checks, but he didn't think anything would show up. She seemed exceptionally clean-cut. Her autistic son was the only cross she seemed to bear. For the moment, at least. He sighed and wondered how he let himself get into these jobs. Maybe his mother had been right all those years ago. Maybe he should have settled down and had a family to occupy his time.

Chapter 9

Two weeks later, Kira sat in front of the warm fireplace, going over the want ads again. The time had flown by with Jared in school, and she had come to the conclusion that finding a job would be a lot harder than she had thought. Not only was she not qualified for most of the part-time jobs that were out there, but aside from the paper, she didn't even really know where to look.

As she stared into the yellow and blue flames, her thoughts wandered to Grant. She wondered how he was and what he was doing. All this time had passed without any word from him. His brothers seemed to be handling the place next door on their own.

"Mom, when can I go work on the tree house with Marcus and Grant?" Jared said, interrupting her thoughts.

"I don't know, Jared. You will have to wait until they call and ask you." Kira sighed, wondering if that would ever happen now. It might be best if Jared simply forgot about it.

"Why can't you just call Grant and ask him?"

"Because Grant is busy working."

"But it's a Saturday!" He frowned. Then he said, "Can I go next door and ask?"

"No, Jared. It's not polite to invite yourself somewhere. And I don't even think he's there. You have to wait until they ask you. I'm sure they will. Thanksgiving is next month. It's just a busy time of year."

"Oh."

"And I mean it, Jared. Even when he's there, you're not to go next door and bother Grant. Do you understand me?" Kira looked pointedly at her son. "Look at me."

"Yes, Mom."

"Okay, then. What are you and Barbara doing this afternoon?"

"Farmers market. She said it's the last one for a long, long time. Then we might make some brownies." Lost to a new subject, Jared forgot the tree house for the time being.

"You better get ready," Kira said. He moved away just as the phone began to ring.

When Kira picked up the phone, she was surprised to hear Mary Lou's voice.

Grant's mother jumped right to the point. "Kira, I have been thinking about you. I may have the perfect situation for you."

"Okay."

"My friend's daughter, Sarah, has started her own interior design shop here in town. She is quite busy and mentioned looking for someone to help part-time in the shop. Someone to answer phones, handle shipments, etcetera. It could be perfect for you. She's just a little older than you. I think you two would mesh perfectly." Mary Lou bubbled on, hardly taking a breath.

Kira finally had a chance to break in. "It sounds great, but is she actually looking to hire someone?"

"Sarah said to tell you to stop by the store if you are interested. It's called *We've Got You Covered,* and it's right downtown."

"Sounds great. I'll go this afternoon. Mary Lou, you're wonderful. How can I ever thank you?"

"Well, I could use some help making pies tomorrow, and Marcus would love it if Jared could come work on the tree house."

"It's a date. We'll be there around ten. Thanks again, Mary Lou."

When Barbara and Jared headed off to run errands, Kira changed from sneakers, jeans, and a t-shirt to knee-high boots, a floral skirt, and a light blue sweater. Then she drove into town.

Kira's nerves started to rattle as she drove into the parking lot of *We've Got You Covered*. As she walked into the quaint shop, she noted the lamps and antiques, fabric swatches, and carpet samples. "I'll be right with you," she heard a voice call out from the back.

Kira nosed around, taking it all in. This was adorable. Pictures on the wall ranged from country décor to Victorian. The shop was cluttered, but cozy.

"May I help you?" An attractive woman with brown hair came around from out back. She approached Kira with a warm smile.

"Hi, I'm looking for Sarah," Kira said.

"I'm Sarah."

"I'm Kira. Mary Lou Rutledge sent me."

"Hi there. Mary Lou told me to expect you. Nice to meet you. Come on back where we can talk." Sarah led the way. "Don't mind the clutter. I just opened the shop about a month ago, and as you can see, I could really use some help sorting things out."

Carefully navigating the piles of unopened boxes, they made their way to a small room in the back. Kira could see that it was filled with samples. She took a seat next to a shipment that appeared to be ready for delivery.

Sarah jumped right into the conversation as they sat down. "Basically what I'm looking for is someone to help me run the shop in the morning, answer phones, and handle shipments that come in when I'm not here. I'm hoping to meet with clients most mornings. In fact, we can work out that schedule together for times when you can be here. Mary Lou said you don't have much work experience, but really, that's okay. What do you think?"

"I think it sounds great! As long as I'm done by two, we should be all set."

"Can you start on the Monday after Thanksgiving, at nine?"

"I will see you then. Thank you."

"You're welcome. Oh, and it's fine to wear jeans as long as they aren't ripped." She patted her own dark blue Levis. "Not a ton of clients actually come into the shop."

Sarah smiled then and led Kira back to the front of the store. "I'll expect you on Monday, and if you have any questions before that, just give me a call."

As Kira drove home, the possibilities of how different life could be now blew through her mind. Things were changing for her and Jared, and though it was a little scary, it was definitely exciting. Once again her thoughts drifted to Grant, and she wondered where he was and why she hadn't heard from him. Was it like him to just run from problems? Maybe he was more like Patrick than she had wanted to believe. Maybe it was a good thing they had had a falling out. She thought, "I will see if Mary Lou drops any hints tomorrow."

* * *

Jared could hardly contain himself as Kira parked the car in the Rutledge family's driveway. The excitement and anticipation of working on the tree house had him in such a state he had reverted to signing.

"Jared, you need to use your words," Kira prompted as she unbuckled him. "Marcus doesn't know sign language. You need to focus and use your voice."

"Okay, Mom," Jared said, but his fingers still moved in conjunction with his verbal response.

Ringing the doorbell, Kira continued to remind Jared to stay calm and to talk without signing so Marcus could understand him.

"I'm so glad you two made it." Mary Lou swung open the door. "Marcus has been getting ready all morning for you, Jared."

"Hi, Mary Lou," Kira said. "That makes two of them who are excited!"

"Come on in. Jared, let's go find Marcus. I think he's out looking at that old tree house just waiting for you."

"Okay," signed Jared.

"Use your words, Jared," Kira said. "He's so excited; he's signing more than talking. I hope it doesn't become a problem for Marcus."

"Don't worry about Marcus. He'll tell Jared to talk to him if he doesn't understand what he's signing. Those two will get along just fine."

As they stepped into the backyard, the coolness of the air was refreshing. Kira breathed deeply, allowing herself to relax. Jared raced off to the tree house, oblivious that Kira was there. She stood back and watched as Marcus spoke quietly to Jared, pointing out everything they would need and explaining what they would be doing in a way Jared could understand.

"I don't think I have ever seen him listen so intently before." Kira was surprised.

"It is amazing what a fun project will do for listening skills. Marcus always said the best way to teach children is to get their attention first. Now, how about those pies?"

"Sounds good. I guess I don't need to worry about Jared. It looks like he'll be well occupied."

Mary Lou was an excellent cook. As the morning progressed, Kira learned about the art of rolling piecrust and the secrets of the Rutledge family apple pie. When Kira was growing up, any pies that made it to their table were straight off the supermarket shelves. She found the whole process a bit overwhelming.

As the pies went in to bake, Kira filled the sink with soapy water and dropped in the dirty dishes.

"How about a cup of hot coffee, Kira?"

"That sounds wonderful."

"Good. After all the hard work, nothing sounds better than a cup of coffee and a heart to heart."

"I'm just going to wash up these dishes while it brews," Kira said.

"I'm assuming the job interview went well?"

"Yes, thank you for that. I start the Monday after Thanksgiving."

"Great. I knew you and Sarah would be a good match." Mary Lou bustled around, starting the coffee.

Kira said, "I think we should get along fine. She seems pretty ambitious, and she's willing to let me wrap up by two so I can still pick up Jared at school."

"That's important." Mary Lou set two coffee mugs on the counter. Then she looked Kira in the eye. "So, Kira, I'm not going to beat around the bush. What really happened that night after we all had dinner together?"

Kira had hoped for some news about Grant, but this question caught her off guard. "What do you mean?"

"I mean that night between you and Grant. One minute he was taking you and Jared home, and the next minute he was storming back in here to say he was leaving for a few weeks. That must have been one hell of a fight. Do you want to talk about it?"

"What did Grant tell you?"

"Not a thing. It's not like him to run away. I don't know what got into him, and I'd like to hear it from you." Mary Lou poured the coffee, sat at the table, and looked directly at Kira again. "So what happened?"

Kira dried her hands and came to the table. "Honestly, Mary Lou, I'm not really sure." She frowned. "Is Grant in the habit of running off when there is a problem?"

"No, he's not in the habit of running off. But it sounds like maybe you expected him to do it. Is that how Patrick was?"

"I . . . I didn't say that."

"Kira, I want to ask you something, and I would like an honest answer. This is between you and me; it will go no further. Did you have a bad marriage with Patrick? Maybe not physically abusive, but was it still a bad marriage?"

Kira stared down into her coffee cup. She could feel the tears gathering. "I don't know how to answer that."

"Honestly. That's all I ask."

Kira took a deep breath. "It wasn't the marriage I was hoping it was going to be. We met when I was only eighteen. I guess I was starry-eyed. My parents were completely out of my life at that point, and I was living with a friend. I had lost touch with my grandfather, who was the only person who had ever truly seemed to love me. I wanted to feel like I belonged with someone again. Patrick was pretty persuasive, and he said he felt the same way, too. His father was already in a nursing home with Alzheimer's, and his mother had died years before that. He had a good job, and he said we'd be all the family we'd need. I really wanted to believe that."

She paused for just a moment. "We moved here when I inherited my grandfather's house. After we were married, I got pregnant pretty quickly, but then Jared was a difficult baby. We didn't have friends, we didn't have family, and Patrick was pretty angry. He wasn't physically abusive, but at home he yelled a lot. Mostly he stayed at work because I couldn't console the baby."

As she continued to stare at her cup, the tears fell, one by one.

Mary Lou reached for her hand. "Of course you couldn't console him. He's an autistic child. But you were married, and your husband should have supported you."

Kira looked up at Mary Lou. "I really needed Patrick to help me, but he thought it was all my fault. He yelled things like 'Get him to stop crying!' and 'Can't you shut him up?' One night when Jared was crying, he yelled,

'What kind of mother are you?' Then he stormed out of the house and took off in his car . . ."

Kira took a deep breath, afraid to continue.

"Go ahead, honey. It's time you said it aloud."

Kira closed her eyes. "When he stormed out of the house that night, I wished he would never come back. I was just so tired and lonely. I had no idea he would have an accident. Oh, God, how could I have known? I didn't mean for it to happen." The tears flowed freely now.

Mary Lou got up, came around the table, and took Kira in her arms. "Kira, it's not your fault. Jared's autism was not your fault, and that accident was not your fault. This guilt and this blame aren't emotions that you should be carrying with you. You're a good mother. You didn't have your husband's support. The wish you had that night was born out of exhaustion and resentment. Any woman would have felt the same way. You did nothing wrong. You have to know that."

As Kira wiped her eyes, she gave Mary Lou a tired smile. "On some level, I guess I do. I just can't help feeling I never should have had that thought. By that time, I was so angry with Patrick for never being around. Never holding Jared, never helping with him. He seemed to resent Jared for needing so much of my time. He acted like a child instead of a father."

"Did Grant say something about Patrick that caused the fight?"

Kira shook her head. "Actually, no. It really was me. Looking back, it probably was a stupid fight. He asked me a question, and I got defensive."

"What question?"

"He asked why I don't have any photos of Patrick on my mantle."

"Oh. Well, that's just none of his business." Mary Lou stood up. "I know I can be a bit of a nosy parker, but I thought I had taught that son of mine better manners."

"It's not really his fault, Mary Lou. I've had plenty of time now to think about it. When you look at it from Grant's point of view, he knows what a good marriage looks like. Heaven forbid, if something were to happen to Marcus, you wouldn't pack up your pictures of him. I think that's all he was expecting." Kira watched Mary Lou for a reaction.

"Maybe you're right, but I still think it's your business. He pushed you for an answer, and you pushed him away because you were scared. He probably figured, 'She wants some space? I'll show her some space.' He's just like his father—stubborn as a mule."

Kira laughed aloud. Finally some of the tension was broken. "Well, it's good to know where he gets it. Seriously, though, I guess I should have explained my reasoning for putting the photos away. But I didn't know how he would react to—"

"I know Grant, Kira. He wouldn't judge you for it. In fact, he'd be angry with Patrick for not supporting you. But honey, if you and Grant are going to be a couple, then you will need to work through it. I can't tell you how, and obviously my son is stubborn."

She continued, "The truth is, he's not one to say much to me about his love life. All that time he was in Texas, I'm not really sure what was going on. It seemed like there was someone, but clearly it didn't work out. This isn't to justify the fact that he went away after your fight. All I'm saying is that he probably has some of his own battle scars, too. Maybe it's time to take down some of your barriers and let him in . . . if you think you care for him. You can't keep pushing him away if you want this relationship to grow."

Kira sighed. Could she care so deeply for a man she hadn't known that long? She sipped her coffee thoughtfully. "Where is he?"

"He's gone up the coast to look at a piece of property. There's a lot to oversee: surveying, ordinances, and so forth. But he'll be back for Thanksgiving. In fact, I would like to invite you, Jared, and Barbara here for Thanksgiving. Will you come?"

"I don't know. Jared's not used to big commotions. You know, with a lot of people around. It's usually just the three of us."

"You just need to tell me what he requires. You can't always stay home. You need family too. Just promise me you will talk it over with Barbara."

"Okay, I promise. Barbara really likes your family, and her sisters can't come for Thanksgiving this year. Really, Barbara has been the true godsend through all of this. Did you know that she used to work for my grandfather? After Patrick was killed, she contacted me. It was such a relief to reconnect with her. And she's been with us ever since."

Before they could say anything else, Marcus and Jared came into the kitchen, cheeks red from the cold. Jared, grinning from ear to ear, climbed into Kira's lap and placed his head on her shoulder.

"Marcus taught me how to hammer a nail today!" Jared burst out. "He let me do it all by myself. I got to hold the hammer. I didn't even hit my hand."

"Good for you, Jared." Kira and Mary Lou exchanged smiles.

"I bet you used that small red hammer," Mary Lou said.

"Yeah, how did you know?"

"That was Grant's hammer from when he was a kid. Marcus gave it to him so he could help his dad with projects."

"Cool. I can't wait to tell him I got to use his hammer." Jared yawned. "We also made a window and put it in a new wall."

"Jared is quite the handyman," Marcus said. "The best thing Jared does is listen very carefully before he does anything. I was quite impressed, Kira. He's a smart boy around tools."

"Thank you, Marcus. I appreciate your taking time with him."

"Marcus used a snapping string that leaves blue lines. That shows me where to hammer the nails," Jared said, sleepily.

"Chalk line," Marcus injected.

Jared yawned again.

"I guess that's my cue to get this young man home. Thank you for tiring him out. He'll definitely sleep tonight."

"He had a great time. I told him we could finish it up on Thanksgiving morning, if that's okay with you?" Marcus said.

"I guess we'll be here for Thanksgiving, Mary Lou. I'm sure Jared will insist now." Kira smiled. "Thank you both. You've been wonderful with him."

"We've already come to love you both, and we enjoy every second you're here." Mary Lou reached for Kira's coat as Marcus picked up Jared to carry him to car. "He's like the grandson we don't have. Bring him by any time."

Chapter 10

Kira awoke Thanksgiving Day with a wave of trepidation. It was the first time in years that she would have Thanksgiving with another family. Of course, Barbara had been all for it. She had simply reminded Kira that it was good for Jared to spend time with other people.

Kira groaned as she rolled out of bed. She parted the curtains and thought, "Am I more afraid of Jared's reaction to the crowd for the day, or my own reaction to seeing Grant?

She pulled a pink chenille sweater out of the closet and found a skirt to match. She wondered if Grant would even notice that she had dressed up. As she picked out some earrings she heard Jared rushing around the living room. He and Barbara were discussing the tree house. He sounded so excited. She realized how much Jared had taken to Mary Lou and Marcus, and they to him. But what if there was another falling out? This was one of the reasons she had, for so long, protected Jared and herself from getting involved with anyone.

"Happy Thanksgiving," Kira said, entering the living room.

"Happy Thanksgiving to you. You look great, Kira." Barbara smiled.

"Hi, Mom," Jared said. "Can we go now?"

"No, it's too early, Jared."

"Marcus said we could work on the tree house this morning. I'm all ready."

"I know. You've been up for hours ready to go. How about some sensory therapy before we go to prepare you for the day. Their entire family is going to be there, and it will be quite noisy." Kira got out Jared's therapy mat and laid it out on the floor. "Come on. Sensory therapy will help you through the day. After that we'll get together some stuff to take with you to use while we're there in case you get overloaded."

"Okay, Mom. But then can we go?"

"Yes, after we're done."

While Jared and Kira went through the joint manipulations to help his sensory system come together and keep him more focused as his senses got more overloaded, she cued him as to what his routine might be like for the day. Knowing she couldn't totally prepare him, Kira reminded him to come to her throughout the day if he felt he needed more therapy.

When they were done, she said, "Now let's get your sensory travel bag together. What do you think we should take today?"

Jared scurried around, picking out his vibrating star, some Matchbox cars and his weighted vest. Finally they met Barbara in the hall and walked out to the car together. During the drive to Marcus and Mary Lou's house, Jared talked all the way, barely signing at all.

As they entered the house, Barbara inhaled deeply. "Now, this smells like a good old-fashioned Thanksgiving."

Jared scampered off toward the kitchen, with Kira and Barbara close behind. From the doorway, they could hear Mary Lou laughing.

"Now, Marcus, I'll tell you one more time. Keep your fingers off my food. There will not be enough for dinner if you keep picking at it!"

"Marcus, Mary Lou!" Jared raced over to hug them.

"Jared, you're here!" Mary Lou returned Jared's hug. "Take this old man out of my kitchen, would you? He keeps snatching all the treats."

Marcus folded Jared into a bear hug next. "Let's go work on your tree house, my boy, and leave these womenfolk to do what they do best . . . cook." Marcus ducked as Mary Lou threw a dishcloth at him. He continued, "So, how's it going today, Jared?"

"Good. I got up early to come, but Mom made me do therapy first."

"That's a good thing. If you need to do more, we'll find a quiet spot. You just let us know."

"Okay."

Kira watched as the pair headed out to the tree house, Jared's small hand in Marcus's large one. She thought, "Marcus has been so good for him. He's never had a grandfather." Then she swallowed hard and choked back the tears. "Pull it together, girl. Don't go all sentimental."

She took a deep breath and turned back to Mary Lou. "What can we do to help?"

"Well, turkey's in. Potatoes need peeling."

"I can do that," Barbara said. "This is great. Just like the hours I've spent with my sisters. Nothing makes the holiday more special than a kitchen full of women working together to make Thanksgiving dinner ."

"I know what you mean, Barb," Mary Lou agreed. "Years you do it alone, it gets kind of lonely in the kitchen. I love having company while I cook."

"We smell something good to eat." Two young men walked in but stopped dead in their tracks upon seeing that Mary Lou wasn't alone.

"Boys, you remember Barbara O'Donnell. And this is Kira Nichols. Her son, Jared, is out with Dad working on the tree house. These are my younger sons, Samuel and Brandon."

"Nice to meet you," Kira said.

"Heard a lot about you," Sam said. He pushed a lock of curly dark hair off his forehead and gave her an impish grin.

Brandon reached out a hand. He looked like a younger version of Grant. Kira noticed that he even had the same cleft chin and deep blue eyes.

"Hi, nice to finally put a face with the name," Brandon said.

"Really? All good, I hope."

"Oh, yeah. And just as beautiful as Grant said."

Sam jabbed his brother in the ribs as Brandon turned to their mother. "Looks like you don't need our help, Mom. We should probably go tackle the tree house with Dad and Jared. Nice to see you again, Barb."

As the young men made a quick escape, Kira overheard Brandon say, "Wait 'til Grant gets home!"

She turned to Grant's mother. "Mary Lou, Grant does know we're going to be here, doesn't he?"

"Um, I think I mentioned it to him."

"You think?" Kira frowned. "That's not fair, and you know it."

"Oh, pshaw," Mary Lou said. "When you two get in the same room and get a chance to talk, you'll do fine. You just need to be honest like you were to me the other day. Open up to him, Kira, and let him know how you really feel."

Mary Lou paused and then offered an apologetic smile. "I know I probably was a little sneaky in all this, but I know you two care for each other, and I have come to love that little boy of yours— and you too, for that matter."

Kira put her hands on her hips and frowned. "I'm sorry, Mary Lou, but this isn't fair to either of us. I thought Grant knew I'd be here. I know you have good intentions, but you need to let us work it out our way."

"Point taken. I'll stay out of it from now on. I told you I can be a nosy parker. I really am sorry."

"Okay, you two," Barbara interjected. "Kiss and make up so we can get back to cooking."

Kira gave Mary Lou a hug. "Jared and I have come to love you and Marcus, too. I know you mean well. I just hope your son isn't as pigheaded as you say he is."

Laughter filled the room as they prepared the rest of the dinner. Barbara and Mary Lou were lovingly patient with Kira's lack of experience in the kitchen, even when she accidentally set one of Mary Lou's embroidered napkins on fire.

The boys came back in about half an hour before dinner was to be served. Jared was obviously tired from the excitement and physical activity. Kira helped him wash up, and then he sat on the floor in the corner of the kitchen and got out his cars. He started lining them up, rocking slightly.

"Oh, no. What's happening?" Kira said, watching him. But before Jared could answer, Grant walked into the kitchen.

"I'm home!" he announced to his mother. Then he stopped short, his eyes resting on Kira.

"Welcome home, son." Mary Lou hugged him. "I'm glad you made it."

"Thanks, Mom. I didn't know we were having a houseful this year." Grant walked over and hugged Barbara. "Happy Thanksgiving, Barb."

"And to you, Grant." Barb kissed him on the cheek.

"Happy Thanksgiving, Kira," Grant said gently. He walked over to her and hugged her close. He whispered softly in her ear, "God, I've missed you."

Kira wrapped her arms tightly around him. "Welcome home."

Then Grant walked over to Jared. Sitting down on the floor beside the little boy, he said, "Hi, Jared."

Kira watched as Grant tried to reach her son, who continued rocking, never making eye contact. Grant continued to talk softly to Jared. She couldn't hear what Grant was saying, but then she saw him sign, keeping his hands out where Jared could see them.

Jared slowly lifted his eyes to Grant and signed that he was happy to see him.

Tears filled Kira's eyes. She was not sure how—or why —Grant had learned some sign language, but he had clearly reached her son.

Grant leaned over and kissed Jared on the forehead before he stood up. Then he turned to his mother.

"Mom, I hope you don't mind, but Jared's having a tough time, so I'm going to rearrange the place settings so Kira, Jared, and I can sit in the kitchen for the meal. It will be easier for him."

"Of course, Grant."

During this exchange, Kira could feel the tears begin to run down her face. Now Grant looked at her and asked, "What's the matter, honey?"

"Why, h . . . how . . ."

Grant enveloped her in his arms as Mary Lou and Barbara quietly left the kitchen. "We obviously need to talk, but there's one thing you need to know now. I really care about you and Jared. I just wanted to give you space. Can you see how I'm feeling?"

"Yes, I can see it. Grant, I just—"

Kira looked up at him and Grant bent down and gently kissed her, his lips teasing hers. Kira moaned softly, pushed him away, and closed her eyes. "We can't do this now. It's your mother's kitchen."

Grant chuckled. "Yes, and undoubtedly Mom and Barb are behind that door wondering if everything is okay."

"We still need to talk, though."

"I know. There is a lot of air to clear between us."

As if on cue, Mary Lou and Barbara bustled back into the kitchen, where Mary Lou took charge. "We've got to get dinner on the table, you two. Grant, you set the table in here for you and Kira and Jared. Kira, start getting the vegetables into serving dishes."

Before long, dinner was set out on the tables. Jared was able to tune in thanks to the quieter setting of the kitchen, and he conversed with Grant about the tree house. When the little boy paused to finish his turkey, Grant reached across the table and held Kira's hand.

Once dinner was over, Jared led Grant and Kira outside to check out the tree house. They stood on the lawn and watched him scamper up the ladder.

"It's amazing how much they accomplished in such a short time," Kira said.

Grant agreed. "I miss working with my dad. He taught me so much as a kid."

"He's been so good with Jared. Jared has learned a lot from Marcus."

"Dad speaks highly of Jared. It was great that you brought him over here to work with Dad."

"I had a good time with your mom, too. Your parents are great people. You're lucky to have them, Grant."

Grant turned to face her. "There is still a lot that needs to be said between us, and we can't keep skirting the issues."

"I know. I want to know why you ran away."

"I didn't run away. What are you talking about?" Grant looked amazed.

"After we had that fight, you just took off for this job with no word, nothing. You ran away, Grant. You can't deny that."

"Kira, you had me at arm's length. I was giving you the space it seemed you wanted."

"Space it seemed I wanted? You're the one who stormed out. You pushed and pushed. I told you not to . . . all over some stupid photos. Why couldn't you just let it go?"

"Why couldn't you just tell me? You still can't. You can't let me in at all, can you?" Grant took a step closer to her and their eyes locked.

"It's not that I'm trying to keep you out. There is so much you don't know. Maybe I'm just not ready to talk about it yet. I don't understand why you have to push the issue."

Kira turned and walked a few steps away, looking up to the tree house, watching Jared.

Grant came up behind her and put his arms on her shoulders. He said, "Why do I have the distinct feeling we're beating around the bush still and nothing has changed?"

"Why are you so pigheaded, Grant Rutledge?" Kira turned and walked into the house.

When Jared and Grant came into the kitchen, Kira and Mary Lou were finishing the dishes. Barbara had coffee ready and dessert was on the table. Kira hoped that Grant couldn't tell that she'd been crying.

"I think it's time for me to get Jared home, Mary Lou. It's been a long day for him, and he's pretty overwhelmed," Kira said.

"Are you sure, honey?" Mary Lou asked. "I can pack up some desserts for you."

"Yes, please. This is his first holiday with a big family, and I don't want to overdo it. Thank you so much for having us, though. I loved it." Kira hugged Mary Lou and turned to Barbara. "Why don't you stay awhile. I'm sure Marcus wouldn't mind dropping you off later."

"No, he certainly wouldn't," Mary Lou said. "Sounds like a great idea."

Kira reached for Jared's hand. "Come on, Jared. It's time to go."

Jared avoided her hand and turned to hug Grant. "I want Grant to take me home."

"Not tonight, Jared," Kira said. "We have our own car today. And I'm sure Grant wants to visit with his mom and dad. He hasn't seen them in a while."

Grant placed his hand on Jared's shoulder. "Do as your mom says, Jared. I will see you another night."

Jared went into the living room to say goodbye to the others. He returned to the kitchen and reported that Marcus and Grant's brothers were watching the football game. Grant picked him up and said, "I'll take you out to the car."

After Grant buckled Jared into his booster seat, he gave her a brief nod.

"'Night, Grant." Kira's heart ached. How could this be happening? How could two people have so much chemistry and yet be at such odds?

"'Night, Kira." Then, as he turned to walk back to the house, he added, "Who's doing the running now?"

Chapter 11

Kira dressed carefully for her first day of work. Her hands were clammy as she fastened on earrings. Her stomach tightened as nervousness took hold. She was so grateful that Sarah's flexibility about her schedule had made this all possible.

Fortunately, Jared was relaxed this morning. She dropped him off at the preschool with no problems.

After parking in the municipal lot, Kira gathered her thoughts, squared her shoulders, and entered the store.

"Welcome, Kira," Sarah said.

"Hi." Kira smiled.

"Ready to get started?"

"Sure. Where do I start?"

Sarah laughed and led the way out back. "I ask myself that all the time!" She gestured at the pile of boxes. "For now, an order just came in, so we need to organize that."

For the next few hours, Kira learned about breaking down an order and making sure everything had come in. Time passed quickly. Kira enjoyed the work.

"You're a fast and organized learner. I think we'll make a great team." Sarah wiped her hands and smiled at Kira. "How about some lunch?"

"Great. I'm famished."

"I'll run down to the deli and get some soup and sandwiches. If you could type these invoices into the computer while I'm gone, that would be great. Just open those files I showed you earlier."

"Okay." Kira sat at the computer. Finding the right file, she quickly figured out how to put the invoices in. "Not a bad first day," she thought.

The ringing of the phone startled her. She picked it up and said, "Good afternoon. *We've Got You Covered.* Kira speaking."

"Kira?" The deep voice that came across the line took her breath away.

"Grant. What a surprise. What can I do for you?"

"When you did you start working for Sarah?"

"Today, actually. If you need to talk to her, she will be right back. Is there something I can help you with?"

"I called to set up a time for Sarah to look at the oceanfront house for interior colors. Can you set up the appointment for next week?"

"Yes. She has time next Tuesday at ten. Will you be back in town?"

"Yes, the time is fine. Kira, please can we get together and talk? Things went badly between us on Thanksgiving Day. I really want to clear the air. There have been so many misunderstandings."

Kira sighed. "Grant, is there any point? You send mixed signals. I can't afford for Jared to get attached just for you to be gone one day. It's not fair to him."

"Do you really think I would do that?"

"I don't know. I guess we don't know each other well enough to be sure."

"So the best thing is to push me away and shut yourself apart from any happiness, right?" Grant sounded angry now. "I will be back in town Thursday afternoon. I really would like to see you for dinner. We need to talk. I will call you Thursday." The phone clicked and he was gone.

Kira looked up to see Sarah standing there, watching her. "Everything okay?"

"Fine. You have an appointment Tuesday at ten with Grant Rutledge for some interior colors. His address is in the book."

"Okay. Great first day. I'm pleased with how quickly you've picked up everything. I'm anxious to meet this

Grant. I've only heard about him from his mother. Have you ever met him? I understand he's quite good looking."

"I have met him. This house you're meeting him at is right next door to mine. And he is quite good looking, if you go for that type." Kira got up and started shuffling papers.

"Right next door? Is there something going on between you two?"

"We went out a couple of times. I don't know if I would say there's anything serious. Jared took a real liking to him, but you know how kids are."

"What about you? Did you take a real liking to him?" Sarah seemed to be watching Kira carefully.

Kira shuffled the papers on the desk again, avoiding eye contact. "I'm not really sure how I feel. I'm not sure if Grant can be trusted to stick around."

"Why is that?"

"I'd rather not get into it, Sarah, if you don't mind. He's got his business, which obviously takes him away, and I'm just not sure that is conducive to what Jared needs in his life." Kira stood up.

Sarah spread out their lunch on the desk. "That's exactly how a good mother thinks. You need to put your child first."

Kira sighed. "It's all so confusing at times."

After lunch, they briefly discussed business orders and appointments. Then Kira left to pick up Jared from preschool. On the way over, Kira's thoughts drifted toward Grant again. He had said he would be back in town Thursday. Her stomach clenched in anticipation. Logic told her to break all ties now and stay far away from him. But her heart said she was falling in love with this man, regardless of how logical she wanted to be. Just thinking of him made her pulse race. His voice made her weak in the knees. She was starting to feel like a teenager again.

Shaking her head, she tried to clear her mind, but she couldn't erase the mental image of those sparkling blue eyes and that incredible smile. What was she thinking?

Chapter 12

After talking with Grant, Kira spent the rest of the week in a nervous mood. Would he still be angry when he returned? She needed to explain things, but would she be able to go through with it and bare her soul? How much should she tell him? She knew the answer was *everything*—if she truly wanted to trust him with her heart. The question was, did she want to trust him?

Thursday morning Kira awoke to the sun shining on a crisp fall day. The weather forecaster predicted rising temperatures despite the fact that it was the last day of November. She planned to drop Jared off at preschool, work until two, pick him back up, and then figure out what to wear for dinner. Later, she would prepare Jared to see Grant again. He would be ecstatic.

Work was already serving as a great outlet. She was learning the business, and she loved every minute of it.

She was grateful to Mary Lou for setting her up with Sarah. That morning, time passed quickly. Kira, engrossed in a new order, was startled when the bell over the door rang. Someone must have come into the front of the store.

Kira put aside her papers and stepped out from the back room. "Hello, may I help you?" She froze when she saw Grant standing there, his back to her, admiring a Victorian lamp.

Grant turned. "Just thought I would check out the store since I'll be working with Sarah next week. Hello, Kira."

"I thought I wouldn't see you until tonight."

"Yes. Well, I didn't really give you a chance to finalize plans, did I?"

"No, not exactly. What time were you thinking of?"

"How about six?"

Kira paused before responding. She had been thinking about this all day, and now she knew what she had to do. "Let's make it four. I want to take you somewhere first before it gets dark. Okay if I drive?"

"Okay. Kira, I'm sorry for getting angry. I'm just so frustrated with—"

The bell over the door rang again and Sarah entered.

"Hi."

"Hi, Sarah. This is Grant Rutledge. The contractor you have an appointment with on Tuesday. He stopped by to meet you ahead of time."

"Grant Rutledge, what a pleasure to meet you."

"The pleasure is mine. I will see you Tuesday. I trust you can find the place okay?"

"Yes, not a problem. See you then."

"Great. I'm looking forward to it. See you later, Kira." Grant turned and left the store without a look back.

"So that's Grant? He's a hunk." Sarah winked at Kira.

"Yes, quite the hunk." Kira quickly changed the subject. "The Harrington order is all set, Sarah. I believe you have a five o'clock appointment with them tonight. Should I help you load your car before I take off?"

"That would be great. You've been a godsend already. I honestly don't know how I got along without you."

* * *

As she picked out her nicest pair of jeans and a jade silk shirt, Kira's mind raced. Her fingers trembled as she fastened the buttons. She clenched her hands, trying to calm herself. Did she really want to do this? She had been thinking about this all day and still had no firm answer.

To take Grant out there. Was that where she wanted to tell him everything? Could she view that site again and still hold herself together?

She leaned close to the mirror to apply her makeup and stared at her reflection for a moment. Her eyes had dark circles from the lack of sleep; the emotional strain was apparent in her face. Only careful makeup application would hide the circles. She sighed. She needed to get through this.

At four o'clock on the dot, Grant knocked on the door. Jared raced to let him in. Kira watched from the hallway as Grant picked up Jared, hugging him close. Her heart ached as she observed them. On the surface, Grant appeared to truly care for Jared. Jared truly loved him. A warmth spread through her as she watched them together. She was stunned for a moment to realize that this was the family she wanted. She couldn't let this go.

"Evening, Grant." Kira entered. She had purposely chosen the shirt to bring out the green in her eyes; it hung loosely over her jeans, which she'd tucked into low black boots with two-inch heels.

"Wow, you look great."

"Thank you." She grabbed her purse and keys. "Ready?"

"Can I come?" Jared asked.

"Not this time, honey. Remember, we talked about this. Grant and Mom have some grown-up things to discuss. Next time, maybe, we can take you for pizza."

Kira gave him a big hug and a kiss on the forehead. "Be good for Barbara."

Barbara came into the living room. "I was thinking, Jared, we could make some cookies."

"Okay." Jared's shoulders drooped, but he reached for Barbara's hand.

"You two go have fun," Barbara said.

"Okay. We won't be late," Kira said. "Thanks, Barbara."

After Kira started the car, she fiddled with the radio to find a soft rock station.

Grant broke the silence. "So where are we going?"

"Not far." She felt Grant's eyes on her, but she wasn't ready to talk just yet. In fact, where would she even start? Damn Patrick for doing this to her. She didn't want to have to go through this. Again she was tempted to cut her losses and say goodbye to Grant. But he seemed so kind. And he had been so good with Jared. Deep in her heart she knew that if she really wanted a chance at love, it should be with this man right here next to her.

Kira struggled to keep the tears at bay. Glancing toward Grant, she became aware that he was closely watching her. Her hands gripped the steering wheel. She pulled onto a sharply curved road and found a safe place to park.

"Are you okay?" Grant asked.

"Yes. We're here." Kira got out of the car, walked over to the guardrail, and sat down on one of the posts. Then she looked down, past the extreme drop off, at the sharp rocks and the raging water below.

"Why did we come here?" Grant came up behind her. "Nice view, though."

"Because I wanted to tell you something, and this felt like the right place to do it."

"Okay." Grant walked around and sat next to her. He took her hand. "What is it, Kira? What's going on that you couldn't just tell me at a restaurant?"

Kira stood and took a couple of steps toward the drop off. She felt angry and frightened all at the same time.

"I'm not the same person I used to be, Grant. Barbara says that after Patrick's death I developed a heart of stone."

"But—"

She put up a hand to stop him. "Please, don't say anything, Grant. Let me just get through this. This is the place my life changed forever." Tears spilled over her lashes as she pointed at the edge of the road. "This is where Patrick's car went over the cliff. The guardrail wasn't here back then."

"Oh, my God. Kira—"

"No, Grant. Please. Let me finish. I'm not telling you this for sympathy. I want you to understand why I've been pushing you away. Why I built up the barriers. But you have to let me get this out, because I don't know if I have the courage to do it a second time."

Kira turned back toward the cliff and stared down. "Damn you, Patrick," she whispered.

Then she continued. "I told you earlier that Jared cried all the time as an infant. Patrick couldn't handle it. Basically, the night of the accident, he told me I was a terrible mom. He said he wanted 'that kid' shut up before he got back. His own son! I was so angry I hoped to God he never came back." Kira's shoulders began to shake with her sobs. "But then I thought the accident was all my fault. For years I carried around the guilt that I was responsible for his accident. I talked to your mom about it a while ago. She helped me see some sense. But it's still so hard."

Kira faced Grant. She wiped her eyes, took in a long breath, and let it out. "Grant, I have fallen in love with you. I see you with Jared. You are great with him. I have fun when we're together. I love your family. But that all just scares me to death. I need to protect Jared and myself. I don't want you to run out on us. I can't go through all that again."

Grant reached for Kira and pulled her close. "Oh, my God, Kira. Why didn't you tell me sooner? What a jerk you must have thought I've been. I'm so sorry for running out that night. I've never cared this much for anyone before. My last serious relationship didn't go so well. I didn't want to say or do something wrong to ruin my chances with you."

Grant gently turned her face until her eyes met his. "Kira, I love you. I would never leave you like that. God, I have been so miserable without you these past few weeks."

"Grant. It's—"

He ran his fingers through her hair to the nape of her neck. He cupped his hand there and pulled her close, his lips claiming hers.

Kira matched his passion, pressing against him. She knew at that instant that he understood.

Grant pulled back and looked down at her. "Kira, why didn't you tell me any of this before?"

"I didn't know how. I didn't want your sympathy."

"Okay. I don't feel sorry for you. But I don't want you pushing me away. I'm not Patrick. I'm not going to run away from Jared because he's autistic. I think I have proved to you that I'll still be there for him when things get rough."

Kira smiled. "You've been great with Jared. But it may get harder when he is older. They say it's more difficult at different stages in their life. I can't tell you what to expect, because honestly I don't know myself."

Grant reached for her hand and helped her off the post. "I think first of all we should go get some dinner." Grant kissed her softly. "Then let's talk some more about this. I think we're going to be okay as long as we keep talking."

She squeezed his hand. "Sounds like a plan."

* * *

The man with the binoculars banged his hand on the steering wheel. He couldn't tell why they had stopped on the side of the road to talk, but from their embrace it was pretty obvious that the guy was a potential complication. His client would not be happy when he reported what he had seen. He decided to follow them for the rest of the night. Hopefully something would change. When they left, he pulled out behind them.

Chapter 13

Kira was exhausted when she awoke Monday morning. She and Grant had spent most of the weekend together, taking Jared for walks on the chilly beach and sitting in front of the fire long after he went to bed. They were determined to start fresh. Kira felt elated that she had trusted Grant with her heart, and that he had stayed by her. He had also talked a bit about his own past—including the long-term relationship that had dissolved when he realized his fiancée, an aspiring model, wasn't interested in ever meeting his family or settling down. As they held hands and stared at the flames she had felt safe and secure, a feeling she had never experienced in a relationship before, even with Patrick. It felt good. They had both agreed to take things slowly, despite the long, passionate kisses when it was time for Grant to go home.

On the way to preschool, Jared quizzed her about when they were going for pizza. Kira finally broke down and promised him that they would go tonight. She mentally made a note to call Grant this morning to make sure it was okay with him. She was sure he wouldn't let Jared down.

As Kira walked in through the back door at *We've Got You Covered,* Kira was surprised to hear Sarah speaking with a customer in the front room. She began her work in the back room, not wanting to interfere.

When the phone rang, Kira picked it up and scheduled a client to meet with Sarah on Friday. Then she walked to the doorway to check on Sarah's visitor. If it was going to be a long meeting, then maybe they'd both like a cup of coffee. But as she reached the main showroom, she froze. It couldn't be. Why was she here?

"Kira! I want you to meet our newest client, Charlene Pearson. Charlene, my best assistant, Kira Nichols," Sarah said.

The woman came forward and looked haughtily at Kira through her designer glasses. Kira would have recognized her Chanel No5 anywhere.

"Well, Kira, this would be the last place I would have expected to see you."

"Charlene, what a surprise." Kira heard the disdain creep into her voice. "What brings you to town?"

"Business, of course."

"You two know each other?" Sarah looked surprised.

Kira turned to Sarah, "Yes, we know each other—unfortunately. I'll be in the back if you need me."

As Kira turned and headed for the back, Charlene called after her.

"Oh, Kira, I was going to call you anyway. I have some business to discuss with you."

Kira turned. "Really? I can't imagine what that would be. You haven't had anything to discuss with me—in how many years has it been, *Mother*?"

"Now, Kira, I'm sure we can sit down and talk civilly. How about a cup of coffee after you've done your job?"

"I don't think so. I have to pick up your grandson. Or did you forget you had a grandson, Mother?"

"Oh, right. I do vaguely remember a phone call about him. What was his name, dear?"

"Goodbye." Kira strode out of the room.

A few minutes later, Kira heard the bell as the wind blew the door shut. The weather had shifted over the weekend, and now it was typical for December—clear but cold.

Kira was shaking as she paced back and forth. When Sarah joined her, she stopped short. "What is it exactly that she wanted?"

"She's in real estate. She said she is acquiring an oceanfront property and is going to be redecorating it. Kira, I had no idea it was your mother."

"I know. I haven't spoken to her in years."

"Get your coat. We're taking a much-needed coffee break. Let me close the shop for the next hour or so." Sarah went to the front to lock up and change the *Open* sign to *Closed*.

"Are you sure about this?" Kira asked.

"Absolutely. I don't have any appointments today, and I think a long chat is what you need. Let's go."

They walked down the street to the coffee shop, where they found a quiet booth in the back. They ordered their coffees and settled in. Then they sat in silence for a while as Kira gathered her thoughts.

Finally she said, "Sarah, thanks for this. You can't imagine my shock at seeing Charlene. I haven't spoken to her since Jared was born. I called her to let her know she had a grandson, and she basically said she was too young to be a grandmother. I'm surprised she even allows herself to wear glasses." Kira gave a pained shrug. "I haven't heard from her since."

"What?" Sarah looked shocked. "What grandmother wants nothing to do with her own grandchild?"

"My mother, apparently. But then again, she basically wanted nothing to do with her own daughter. I hardly ever saw her when I was growing up. She was too involved in building up her real estate career. I was an unwanted nuisance who got in the way when she was home. I used to spend my summers here with my grandfather, which was great, but then they had a falling out."

She took a deep breath and continued. "I received more birthday presents from the housekeeper than from Charlene. I spent my birthdays having cake with the housekeeper. Charlene was typically out of town on business or off on one of her business dinners. Christmases were much of the same. Someone usually put something under the tree for me, but she was never around."

"Where was your dad?"

"Typically off drinking somewhere. I think he was trying to avoid her. Eventually they got divorced, and he died a few years back. I left home the day I turned eighteen. I moved in with a girl from school and worked as a waitress until I got married."

"Kira, I'm so sorry. I just can't imagine. I feel so lucky; my own childhood was nothing like that."

"You are lucky, Sarah. From what you've said, you have a great relationship with your mom." Kira gave her boss a tired smile. "I just wonder what Charlene wants. What kind of business could she want to talk to me about?"

"Are you going to meet with her?"

"I suppose it will be inevitable, if there's any hope she'll leave town soon." Kira finished her coffee and stood up. "Now we have work to do. We have wasted enough time this morning on Charlene Pearson, who—believe me—is not worthy of even this amount of time."

As they left the coffee shop, Kira realized that how much it warmed her to be able to talk to Sarah and Mary Lou. Her life was finally expanding to include some friends and family, which she'd never had before.

* * *

Charlene drove around the cul-de-sac of the oceanfront property. God, that private eye was useless. The sign clearly said Rutledge Construction. She parked her rental car and formed her own plan.

There were only two men working on the site, hammering nails into the newly erected walls. Both of the men looked young. She had nothing to lose. Exiting her vehicle, Charlene approached the house, looking around. One of the young men approached her. "Can I help you?"

"I hope so. I'm looking for some information on this beautiful home." She smiled sweetly. "Do you own it?"

"My family does. I'm Sam. You really need to speak to my brother, Grant. He should be back shortly."

"Is it for sale?"

"Like I said, you need to speak with Grant. Is there some way he can reach you?"

"I'm passing through, really. Do you have his business card? Then I can give him a call when I get a chance." Charlene turned and looked toward Kira's house.

"Here you go. Can I tell him you were here?"

"Sure. That will be fine." Charlene took the card and briskly headed for her car.

"Hey, your name?" Sam yelled after her.

Charlene raised her hand and waved as she got in. She threw Grant's card on the seat and smiled—Grant Rutledge. Well, if he chose to be involved with Kira, he would never know what hit him.

Chapter 14

Grant had been making plans all morning. Around noon, he had phoned to ask Kira if he could pick Jared up at two o'clock at the preschool for a surprise. Her voice had sounded oddly strained, but she had promised to call Ms. Cheryl to confirm that Grant had permission to pick Jared up. Then they had agreed that he and Jared would meet her at the pizza parlor at five. As Grant headed to pick Jared up at preschool, his mind was full of ideas of how to court Kira. He was determined to break past her barriers. Her beauty alone took his breath away, but she seemed to have no idea of the effect she had on him.

At the preschool, Ms. Cheryl greeted him at the door. "Welcome, Mr. Rutledge. Kira called to let me know that you would be picking Jared up today."

"Great. It's not a problem then?"

"Not at all. She also dropped off his booster seat. Jared is all set."

"Grant! Why are you here?" Jared flung himself into Grant's arms.

"Hi, Jared. I thought we could go do some Christmas shopping for your mom."

"I know what I want to get her."

"Okay. Let's go then."

As they drove into town, Jared was clearly excited. "Sometimes Barbara takes me shopping, but this will be much more fun!"

"Where do you think we should go first?" Grant asked.

"I want to buy Mom earrings."

"Earrings?"

"Yes. Can we get those?"

"You bet. I know just the store."

Parking the car, Grant said, "Buddy, you tell me if you feel overwhelmed, okay? Then we'll go find a quieter spot."

"Okay, Grant."

As they entered the store, Jared immediately ran to the earring display. He pointed to a pair of wired dangling earrings with three white balls on them. "These are them. They look like snowmen. Those are the ones I want for Mom."

"Are you sure? Don't you want to look around some more?" Grant asked.

"No. Those are the ones I want Mom to have."

"Then those are the ones you shall get her. Should we have them wrapped here? Or should we wrap them at home?"

"Will you help me wrap them at home?" Jared asked.

"Of course. But it has to stay a secret. You can't tell your mom what you bought her."

"I won't." Jared smiled and reached for Grant's hand.

After paying for the earrings, Grant and Jared searched for presents for Mary Lou and Marcus, and then for Barbara from Jared. Jared got more excited with every present he bought. As the time got closer to the dinner hour, the stores grew more and more crowded.

Jared tugged on Grant's arm. Grant looked down and saw that Jared was rocking and repeating the same hand gestures over and over again.

As Grant reached down to pick up Jared, he heard a cold voice from behind. "It's a shame when people bring their handicapped children in public. They really should keep them home."

Grant turned in fury. Behind stood a woman with designer glasses dressed in very expensive clothes. She was looking at Jared with disdain.

Grant gathered Jared in his arms. "Lady, I don't know who you are, but you have a lot of nerve commenting on situations you obviously know nothing about. I hope you and I never cross paths again."

Grant headed for the door with his packages and Jared in his arms. "Let's go meet Mom." As they walked out to the car, Jared settled against him and relaxed.

* * *

Kira arrived at the pizza parlor a little early. Still shaken from her encounter with Charlene, she settled into a quiet booth in the back and collected her thoughts. She looked forward to Grant's strong presence to calm her nerves.

When the bells rang on the evergreen wreath that had been hung on the main door, she looked up and saw Grant and Jared enter. Jared was holding Grant's hand and appeared to be happy. Kira breathed a sigh of relief. She realized she had been a little anxious about their adventure—whatever it was—and how Jared would handle it. It was so tough to let go after doing it alone for so long.

"Mom, we got Christmas presents," Jared exclaimed.

Grant kissed Kira softly. "Are you okay?"

"Yes. It's been a long day. But it certainly looks like you guys had a great time."

"We did!" Jared bounced in his seat. "I bought Mary Lou and Marcus a present, and Grant said he would help me wrap it."

"Really? Did you do my shopping too?" Kira teased.

Jared grew serious. "I can't tell. It's a secret."

"Don't you tease and get it out of him," Grant admonished.

Jared talked through the pizza about shopping with Grant. Kira concluded that even if there had been any issues, they had been quickly resolved and forgotten. She decided not to spoil the dinner by mentioning Charlene. No doubt about it, that woman was bad news.

Chapter 15

Bundled up in a parka, hat, and scarf, Kira sat on the deck enjoying her coffee. It was cold out, but the breeze had stopped, and the sparkling ocean was refreshing to watch. No work today. Sarah was in Boston for a design show, and she had told Kira to take the day off. Barbara was also away; she had gone to Wisconsin for a week to visit her sisters.

A knock at the door at the front of the house startled her from her thoughts. She walked around to the front yard and was surprised to see a car from the county sheriff's department in the driveway behind her Honda. At the door stood a middle-aged, portly man with his hat riding low on his head.

He turned at the sound of her footsteps. "Morning, Ma'am. Are you Kira Nichols?"

"Yes, sir. What can I do for you?"

"These papers are for you, Ma'am. Have a nice day." The sheriff tipped his hat as he turned to leave.

Puzzled, Kira went in through the front door and opened the envelope. She couldn't believe it. It was a summons to vacate the property by December 24th. The papers went on to state that the owner, Charlene Pearson, was insisting the property be vacated by December 24th, as by legal inheritance of the property. Basically, she was claiming that Kira's grandfather had actually left the property to Charlene in a later, recently discovered will.

Kira struggled to take a breath. Her stomach felt like she had just been sucker punched. She leaned against the wall because her knees felt like they might give out at any moment. She closed her eyes for a second, opened them, and blinked. This couldn't be happening.

The papers floated to the floor as Kira stared into space. How could this be possible? There had been a reading of the will after her grandfather's funeral. What was this all about?

Kira slid to the floor and sat there staring at the papers. She felt the overwhelming need to talk to Grant. She picked the papers up and started for the oceanfront property next door. Entering the house, she immediately saw Sam. "Where's Grant?"

"Hi, Kira. What's wrong?" Sam asked.

"I need to talk to Grant. Is he here?" Kira started moving from room to room on the first floor.

"He's upstairs," Sam said.

Kira ran for the stairs. "Grant!"

"What's the matter? Is Jared okay?" Grant ran to the top of the landing.

Kira felt tears running down her cheeks. She pressed the papers into his hands. "I don't understand it."

Grant pulled her close and she wrapped her arms around him as he started reading the papers. "What is this? Where did you get these?"

"The sheriff just served me with them."

"I thought your grandfather left you the house."

"So did I. That's what the lawyer told me at the reading of the will. I don't understand. Why is she doing this, on Christmas Eve?" Kira buried her face in Grant's chest, sobbing.

"It will be okay. I think our first step is to go talk to Dad and have him call Mike Tanger, his lawyer, and see what he says about this." Grant moved her chin gently so she was looking at his eyes. "It will be okay. I'm right here. We'll fight this together. You will not lose your house, babe."

Kira closed her eyes and struggled to regain composure. "I don't know why I burst into tears like that." She wiped the tears away.

"I do. It's a blow, but it's okay." Grant kissed her. "Let's go talk to Dad about this."

As they arrived at the Rutledge home, Grant stopped Kira outside. He pulled her close and held her for a moment. Kira snuggled close and embraced the strength he offered her.

"You ready?" he said.

"We can't just stay like this forever?" She sighed, her head against his chest.

Grant groaned. "How I would like to. Someday, baby, someday."

Holding Kira's hand, Grant led the way into the house. They found Marcus in his study and explained the situation.

Marcus read through the papers and said, "Let's call Mike and see what he thinks about this. Kira, do you still have your copy of the will?" He reached for the phone.

"I don't know." She faltered. "I still have boxes of my grandfather's papers and stuff packed away with Patrick's. Maybe my grandfather's lawyer would still have a copy."

Kira walked to the window and looked out. She listened as Marcus talked with his lawyer and explained the situation. She wrapped her arms around herself, feeling cold. Grant came up behind her and held her.

"It'll be okay, Kira." Grant squeezed her tight. "I think Dad's on the right track."

"I just can't figure out why Charlene would do this, to her own grandson. I can't believe she found a new will after all these years—or that my grandfather would leave her anything." Her voiced trembled as she fought to hold back the tears that threatened once more.

Marcus cleared his voice as he hung up the phone. "Kira, Mike has a couple of suggestions. He would like to meet with you in the next couple of days. In the meantime, he wants you to see if you have the will. If not, he can contact the lawyer who handled the reading. But can you also try to find any papers that might have your grandfather's original signature? Mike is going to request the will that Charlene claims to have so that he can compare signatures."

"Okay. I'll start looking."

"If you find the will, Grant can fax it over to Mike so he can have it for your meeting. Don't worry, honey, we'll do what we can to help you." Marcus came around his desk to envelope Kira in a big bear hug.

"Thank you, Marcus. I don't know what I would do without you all."

"It's what family does, honey. And you and Jared are family. We're not going to let anything happen to you, or let anyone take your house."

"I don't know how to thank you."

"No thanks necessary. Just concentrate on doing what you have to do to get through this, and enjoy Christmas." Marcus kissed her on the forehead.

Grant gave Marcus a hug. "Thanks, Dad. I knew we could count on you."

Chapter 16

Kira walked into the house, shoulders squared and determined to beat Charlene at her own game. She wasn't sure exactly what game Charlene was playing, but she was bound that her mother would not displace her and Jared from their home.

Grant had gone to the oceanfront house to pick up a few things. He'd promised to come over in a few minutes. She started for the back spare room, which was where she had stored all the boxes with her grandfather's papers and Patrick's things.

She stopped in the doorway. She hadn't been in the room since the day she packed Patrick's clothes away. The room smelled musty. She took a deep breath and once again mentally cheered herself on. Crossing the room, she opened the window a crack to let in some fresh air.

The boxes were lined up against the back wall. She had meticulously marked each one: paperwork, clothes, photos, miscellaneous. Some were marked *Granddad* and some were marked *Patrick*. Really, she should give away Patrick's clothes. Someone could probably use them.

Kira immediately went to the box marked as *Granddad's paperwork*. She had not really paid much attention to the content of the material she had placed in this particular box.

Yellow papers and envelopes, and the stale smell of old documents, greeted her when she sat on the floor and opened the flaps. She had no idea what she was looking for. Marcus had said to look for a copy of the will, and something with her grandfather's signature.

She still couldn't believe it was possible that he had made a later will. But would her mother lie about something like that? She sighed. Anything seemed possible with Charlene.

Kira shuffled through papers. Most were just work notes that meant nothing to her. She could probably throw them away. After going through half the box, she still hadn't come across anything like what she needed. What would have his signature on it?

"I'm here, Kira." She heard Grant moving around in the kitchen. "I was going to make some coffee. Do you want some?"

"Sounds good. I'm in the back room," she answered.

She opened a box that didn't seem to have a label. There on top sat their wedding picture. Kira and Patrick. She picked it up. They had seemed to be happy enough at one point. But they hadn't ever really had much in common except for their loneliness. Then everything had changed when Jared was born. She had expected that he would love Jared—and maybe he had, in his own way. But looking at his picture now, she felt nothing—nothing but sadness for a man who obviously had been so shut down inside that he couldn't appreciate what he had right in front of him. A lone tear ran down Kira's cheek. Not for a life with Patrick that she missed, but for the true love she had longed for and never had.

Kira, sensing Grant's presence, glanced up as she replaced the photo back in the box.

"Having a tough time?" Grant handed the coffee over to her.

"Not in the way you're thinking, I'm sure, Grant." Kira smiled and brushed away the tear. "Thank you for the coffee."

"What do you mean? It's okay to miss Patrick."

"That's just it. I don't miss him. I was just thinking how sad it was. It wasn't a partnership filled with love like people long for in a marriage." Kira turned from Grant, suddenly self-conscious about sharing how her marriage really had been.

"Kira, I'm sorry. I had no idea."

"I know. It's one of the reasons it's hard for me to open up. Anyway, I haven't found anything. No copy of the will, and no signature as of yet. After Patrick and I moved in, we did ship a box with some of my grandfather's personal things to Charlene, but I don't recall exactly what we sent. Patrick packed it up for me. She never even acknowledged receiving it."

"Okay. Keep looking. I'll help, if you want. I can look through your grandfather's things, but I don't want to intrude into Patrick's stuff."

"You're not intruding at all. I want your company."

Grant pulled Kira close and kissed her softly. "You are an incredible woman. You are strong for what you have been through and for the way you have handled it. I love you."

Her eyes filled with tears again. "I love you, Grant."

They spent the next two hours poring through the boxes but came up with no sign of the will. Eventually, Kira did find several documents with her grandfather's signature. After putting all the boxes back in order, they closed the room back up.

"I need to get rid of most of that stuff," Kira said as they headed toward the living room. "It's time."

"When you're ready. There is no rule that says you have to clean out stuff in a certain timeframe."

"When do I need to meet with Mike?" Kira asked.

"I'll set up a time now that you have the signature. I faxed the eviction papers before I came over here. Do you want me to go with you when you meet with him?"

"Yes, if you would. I know this really doesn't involve you, but I would feel better if you were there."

Grant took her hand and squeezed it. "I will be there, by your side, every step of the way. I'm not going anywhere."

* * *

Mike's office was actually a small, cape-style house that had been remodeled into an office building. Kira felt instant warmth and comfort when she walked through the doors. The receptionist informed them that Mike would be with them shortly and led them to a small conference room where they could wait.

Kira sat down and started to fiddle with the papers in front of her. "How long do you think we'll have to wait?" she asked Grant. "I told Sarah I'd come back to the shop as soon as we're done."

"It won't be long." Grant reached for her hand. "Mike never keeps my dad waiting long. Relax, Kira, things will work out. Mike seems like a laid-back guy but he's right on top of things. Wait and see what he says."

"I'm so nervous. What if we can't get a court date to fight the eviction before the time we have to be out of the house? What am I supposed to tell Jared? He wants to set up a tree this weekend."

"It will work out," Grant reassured her.

The door opened and in walked a heavyset man in his late fifties. He gave Kira a warm smile. "Kira. Grant. Sorry to have kept you waiting. I was on the phone with Dick Ritzer, Charlene's attorney."

Kira tightened her grip on Grant's hand. She kept her eyes on Mike as he slowly settled into a chair and looked at the papers in front of him.

"Okay," he said. "It seems to me Charlene is the only one who claims to have seen this second will. She says she just found it in a box of your grandfather's things. Dick is waiting on Charlene to get him the original papers so he can get me copies. Right now he doesn't have them."

"What does that mean?" Kira asked.

"Well, right now it means that we will file for a motion to dismiss the eviction based on lack of evidence. If they don't provide us with the documentation, we can subpoena it. If, for some reason, there is no documentation, chances are she will drop the whole thing unless she wants to face charges." Mike leaned back in his chair.

Kira looked at Grant. "What do you make of all this?"

"I think Mike has a good handle on it. If Charlene's attorney doesn't even have the papers, then it seems like she's bluffing. I think you're in good shape to get the eviction notice dismissed."

"How long will that take?" Kira asked Mike.

"I will file the motion for dismissal today and have it filed expeditiously. Hopefully it will go through immediately. The Court Clerk is a good friend of mine. With any luck I will know something for you within a day or two."

"Okay," Kira said. "I guess we'll wait to hear from you."

Mike gave her a warm smile. "Kira, it will work out fine. I don't envision any problems with this one." He rose, offered his hand to each of them, and then showed them to the door.

As they headed for the car, Grant put his arm around Kira. "Let me come get you after work. I think maybe taking Jared to look for a Christmas tree is something we need to be doing. Christmas is only a few weeks away."

Kira felt herself relax for the first time in hours. "Sounds good to me."

Chapter 17

Charlene stood at the sliding glass door in her hotel room and gazed out over the ocean. It was a beautiful view. The peaceful waves rolling onto the shore reminded her of her youth. She had loved being at the ocean with her parents, especially her dad. He would spend hours with her jumping waves and running from them. The ache in her heart for better times tugged at her sometimes. But they had had that huge falling out when he had suggested—no, pushed—that she should spend more time with her daughter. Her heart hardened again. That had been the end of that.

Shrugging her shoulders, she returned her thoughts to the present. It was completely unfair that her daughter had managed to land one of the best locations in this town. But soon it would be hers. Kira wouldn't have a clue what to do with that summons. She always was a spineless girl with no fight. By the end of the week Kira would be handing over the keys to the house. She'd be too intimidated to even wait until Christmas Eve. Unless that young man from the construction site helped her out. What was his name? Oh yes, Grant.

A meeting might be the perfect thing to push Kira in the right direction. Charlene warmed to the idea. Just maybe she would give Kira a surprise visit. She could bring her grandson an early Christmas present. This would also get her an inside view of the house, which she suspected was in major need of redecoration. Kira wouldn't have the nerve to turn her away at the door.

Charlene made a quick stop to the local department store and headed to the toy section. How old was that kid again? Well, what mattered most was to have something in hand. The leftover summer items were marked as clearance on a small shelf at the back of the store. No point throwing much money at this. At the register, she paid cash for the pair of plastic swimming fins and headed back to the rental car.

The road followed the coast, and the sunlight on the waves was gorgeous. Her mind wandered back to when Kira was a child. Thank God for housekeepers and nannies. Charlene had never spent a lot of time with her daughter. She was too busy trying to build her career, and her husband was always off somewhere with his drinking buddies. Kira's grandfather had clearly favored the girl, but after their big blowup, she had never let him see Kira again.

Charlene was proud of the way she had built her career. Her father had never understood that. She was well known as a barracuda in the real estate world, and she always succeeded in getting what she wanted. But for the past few years she had really resented the fact that her father had left Kira the house. Well, not for long.

When Charlene reached the cul de sac, she pulled her thoughts to the present and collected her composure. She put on her game face and started to the front door. Amazed at the Christmas music and sounds of laughter coming from the house, Charlene stopped short. Could it be that Kira was actually preparing for Christmas here in this house?

The door was opened by a handsome, rugged man. Charlene could only presume he was the infamous Grant Rutledge from the construction site next door. "Can I help you?"

"Yes, I'm here to see Kira."

"Do I know you?" Grant frowned. "You look awfully familiar."

"I don't think so. Is Kira here?" Charlene tried to look past the broad shoulders that were blocking her view.

"Who is it, Grant?" Kira approached the door but stopped short when she saw Charlene. Charlene felt her composure slip. Jealousy struck like a freight train; she shook it off.

"Kira, you *are* home." Charlene took one step inside before she was cut off by Grant, who moved in front of her.

"Charlene. What are you doing here?" Kira's voice was cold.

Charlene had expected the cool welcome, but she hadn't expected her daughter to be holding her own. She figured Kira would be worn down and in tears by now.

Grant spoke next. "Charlene? Well, I must say you certainly are exactly what I expected."

"What is it you want?" Kira asked.

Charlene smiled sweetly. "I brought your son an early Christmas present."

"Not interested," Kira said. "And you're not welcome here. You may take your present and go back home. I don't know what you're up to, but I'm not playing your games."

Kira closed the gap between them. "If you have something to say to me, call my lawyer." As Charlene watched, Kira seemed to grow more and more confident. Caught off guard by Kira's forcefulness, she took a step back and found herself just outside the door again.

"Goodbye, Charlene." With a quiet snap, the door shut in her face.

Charlene stood on the walkway. When on earth did her daughter grow a backbone? Well, this would not be the last Kira heard of Charlene. She headed for her car. What she really needed now was a new strategy.

Her cell phone rang as she started onto the road. Based on the caller ID, she could tell it was her lawyer.

"Charlene speaking. Tell me you have good news."

"Well, we are scheduled to meet with your daughter and her lawyer in the next few days."

"Oh, that is good. She is ready to sign over the house?"

"Not exactly. You have been ordered to produce the new will. You could be facing charges, Charlene, if this is not legal." The warning was clear, although he had never questioned any of her legal moves before.

"Relax. Everything is fine." Charlene chewed her bottom lip. Providing authentic-looking paperwork might pose a problem. She had some thinking to do.

* * *

Kira was floored that her mother had the nerve to show up on her doorstep. The audacity of that woman! She moved to the living room and started picking up the mess from decorating the tree. Jared had gone to his room, needing some down time after such a change in routine.

"Are you okay, Kira?" Grant asked.

"Yeah. I can't believe she had the nerve to show up here."

"I had no idea that was her. Do you think we should call Mike?"

"Should we?"

"She shouldn't be showing up on your doorstep after serving you with an eviction notice. Should I give him a call?"

"Yes, that might be a good idea. I don't want Jared anywhere near her." Kira closed up the empty decoration boxes and stacked them against the wall.

Grant finished his phone call with Mike and then smiled and pulled Kira close. "Mike thinks—and I agree—that Charlene is a little unsure of her next move."

"What do you mean?" Kira searched Grant's eyes.

"You and Mike will meet next Tuesday at ten with Charlene and her lawyer. She supposedly will have the copy of the new will. Mike said to tell you not to worry; he thinks things are going very much your way right now."

"What a relief."

* * *

Charlene walked into her hotel room just as the cell phone rang again. This time the caller ID indicated that it was the private detective. A smile curled her lips as she picked it up on the third ring.

"Just the voice I wanted to hear. Do you finally have something good for me?"

"I think you will be pleased with what I found."

"I'd better be, if you think you're going to get paid."

"Listen, lady, I've been in the business a long time. From what you've told me, what I've found is plenty to help you out, assuming that a major part of your plan is some sort of revenge. The guy she is with is Grant Rutledge. He is co-owner of Rutledge Construction, a family-owned business—"

"That's it?" Charlene interrupted. "*That's it?* It took me two seconds to find this out!"

"No, that's *not* it." His voice was cold now. "The rest of the information is in an envelope at the front desk. I expect the money to be wired to my account within an hour or I may have a chat with your lawyer myself." The line went dead.

Charlene collected the envelope and returned to her room. Sitting on the edge of the bed, she let out a slow breath. This could be the moment that would clinch the deal with Kira, pushing the house right into her hands.

Turning the envelope over, Charlene nudged the contents out. She read them slowly and thoroughly. No, they wouldn't help her get the house. But yes, revenge was definitely back on the table. Her daughter would certainly be floored when she found out just what was in Grant's past.

Chapter 18

Kira woke Tuesday morning to the first snowfall of the season. The sky was dark and gray. "Great," she thought sarcastically. "Perfect weather for the day I'm about to have."

She planned her outfit carefully. Facing off against Charlene would be a test of wills both literally and figuratively. Mike might think she was in a good position legally, but Kira had no doubt that Charlene would have something else up her sleeve. Kira needed to be mentally prepared—or at least look the part. She was, after all, Charlene's daughter.

As a child, Kira had watched her mother dress in what she had termed her "power clothes." Charlene had been ruthless in all aspects of her business. Kira had learned one thing from Charlene: dress to impress. Now it was

Kira's turn to strike back—strengthened by the extra fierceness that comes with a mother's love for her son.

Kira took a final look in the mirror. She had dressed conservatively in black pants and a jade sweater. Her black-heeled boots added a few extra inches to her height. Satisfied, she went to make sure Jared was up and getting ready for school.

"Mom, no school today," Jared said when Kira entered the room. He was staring out the window that overlooked the deck, mesmerized by the weather.

"He's dying to get out there," Barb said. "And there really is no school. They just announced it on the news."

Kira joined Jared at the window. "It is really coming down. I don't look forward to driving into town in this."

"Should you call Mike and see if the meeting is still on?" Barb asked. "The roads must be bad if school has been cancelled."

"I'll give him a quick call."

The phone rang as Kira reached for it. "Hello?"

"I'm on my way to pick you up." Grant's voice was on the other end. "Don't drive in this stuff."

"I was just going to call Mike to make sure we are still having the meeting."

"I already talked to him. Charlene insists on having it. She thinks you won't show and then she can move up the eviction. I'm on my way."

"Thanks, Grant. Drive carefully."

Kira filled Barb in while she waited for Grant.

* * *

It was a slow ride into town, but Grant pulled into the parking lot on time.

"Thank God that ride is over." Kira breathed a sigh of relief. "Thanks, Grant, for doing this. I really appreciate it."

"My pleasure. Ready to knock 'em dead?" He reached over and squeezed her hand.

"No, but let's do it." Kira smiled but her stomach was full of butterflies.

Mike greeted them in the reception area. "Nasty weather out there. Glad you made it okay."

"Thank God for four-wheel drive." Grant shook Mike's hand.

"Kira, we're all set if you're ready. I'm not too worried. Charlene's lawyer doesn't seem very prepared." Mike led the way to the conference room.

"We shall see. I don't trust Charlene for an instant." Kira gave Grant's hand a quick squeeze as Mike opened the doors.

Kira squared her shoulders and tried to look calm. She recalled how her mother would act as she left the house for a meeting. The word *steamroller* came to mind. She decided to walk in ahead of the men and take charge immediately.

"Good morning, Charlene, Mr. Ritzer. Such a shame you had to come out in this weather."

"Good morning, Kira, darling." Charlene adjusted her Hermes scarf. "We weren't sure you would make it this morning."

"Then you don't know me that well, Charlene." Kira sat down gracefully directly across from her mother. "I wouldn't have missed this for the world."

Out of the corner of her eye, Kira saw Mike wink at Grant. Then the men came to the table and chose seats to each side of her.

"Well, I guess we should get started." Mike opened his folder. "Now, Charlene, we are looking for the new will you say gives you ownership of the property in question."

"Yes. It is in my home. My *other* home," she corrected herself as she smiled brightly. "Perhaps we can reconvene after the holidays."

"You were supposed to produce it here at this meeting today," Mike said impatiently. He turned to Charlene's lawyer. "Mr. Ritzer, you had agreed to make your client understand that it was imperative she produce the papers today or the eviction would be dropped."

"You can't just drop the eviction!" Charlene said.

He lawyer frowned at her. He turned to Mike and

said, "Mr. Tanger, if I could have just a few minutes alone with my client?"

"Sure."

Kira, Grant, and Mike left the conference room. Kira paced the hallway as the men talked about how Charlene appeared to have blown this one. Grant said, "Clearly this is all over now."

Kira stopped in front of them. "Don't be so sure. Charlene had a pretty smug look on her face. I think she has something else up her sleeve. Can we stop the eviction without the papers?"

"We can. But if she has something else up her sleeve, then it will be another set of problems." Mike shrugged.

"I know Charlene. She doesn't give up that easily." Kira started pacing again.

Her mother's lawyer opened the door. "We're ready now, I believe."

Kira filed into the conference room and stood behind a chair. "Are we ready to proceed, or has this been a waste of our time, Mother?"

Dick Ritzer said, "Charlene, at this time, has decided to withdraw her eviction process."

"No leg to stand on—well, that's a surprise." Sarcasm dripped from Kira's voice.

"No, Kira. I decided that you have been through enough. You and Jared." Charlene spoke softly.

"Yeah, right. I don't believe that for a second. You don't have a generous or kind bone in your body."

Mike broke in. "Well, Dick, if that is the case, you and I can work out the legalities, and everyone else can get going. I'm sure the roads aren't getting any better,"

"Of course. Kira, Grant. Sorry to have dragged you out in the mess." Charlene's lawyer extended his hand to each of them.

"It seems my mother has had you running in circles, Mr. Ritzer. It's a shame you don't pick your clients a little more discreetly." Kira released his hand quickly and then turned to face Charlene.

"I hope you've had your fun, Charlene. It's time you returned home and left us alone for good."

"There is something else I want to talk to you about before I leave," Charlene said. "It is rather important."

"Are you serious? After all this, could there possibly be anything left to say between us?"

"Please, Kira. It's important. And I promise—if it's what you want, it will be the last time you hear from me."

Kira looked at her mother and sighed. "I will be at work tomorrow. You may stop by on your way out of town. I'll give you five minutes. Not a minute more." Then she turned and left the office without a backward glance.

* * *

Charlene slammed the hotel door. She kicked off her shoes and started pacing on the plush carpet of her hotel room. She had been taken aback by her daughter's confidence. She walked to the windows, looked out at the falling snow, and sighed.

Her desperation grew. It wasn't a question of money—she simply wanted that oceanfront house. Her father had built it, and if not for that stupid argument about Kira, it would have been hers. But no, he had always loved Kira more than he'd ever loved her. First he had questioned her parenting skills, and then he had slapped her again by leaving the house to Kira.

The "new" will had seemed like the perfect plan. She had been so sure that Kira would fall for it. The private eye had indicated that the coast was clear—and then she had hooked up with that construction guy. He had obviously backed her. He had probably even found that lawyer for her.

As she moved from the window, the manila envelope on the table caught her eye. No, she wasn't out of the game yet. If she couldn't be happy, then Kira couldn't either. Plain and simple. She still had one more chance at ruining her daughter's life.

Chapter 19

As Kira quickly dressed in a wool sweater and jeans on Wednesday morning, her mind was racing. What could Charlene want to talk about?

She had trouble concentrating even as she helped Jared with sensory therapy to get him focused for school. She rushed him through his maneuvers and prodded him to eat more quickly than usual.

Finally, Kira dropped Jared off with Ms. Cheryl and drove to *We've Got You Covered*. Taking a deep breath, she entered the store, hoping it would be a while before Charlene showed up.

Sarah was already there, unpacking an order. She stopped to ask, "How'd it go yesterday?"

"Conveniently, Charlene 'forgot' to bring proof about the new will. Her lawyer convinced her that the only thing to do was withdraw her request for eviction. Basically that means it's over. I'm sure there's no new will." Kira smiled for just a moment and then frowned. "However, she asked to talk with me here today before she leaves town."

"Why?"

"I have no idea. She didn't say, but I'm sure she has something else up her sleeve." Kira sat down at the desk and started going through the past day's sales receipts to put in the computer.

"You're just going to start work and that's it? Like nothing is going on?"

"What do you want me to do, Sarah? Pace the floor and wait for her to show up?"

"Well, no, not exactly. I just don't know how you do it —stay so calm. I would be a nervous wreck." Sarah went back to unpacking the order.

"I can't sit and worry about this stuff all day." Kira gave a nervous laugh. "That's what I did all night. And got nowhere. Besides, worrying won't get this order together for your appointment, now will it?"

Kira gathered boxes together to pack up the samples Sarah would need. The time flew by quickly. Kira was startled when the doorbell chimed, signaling the arrival of a customer. But Kira didn't have to look up to know Charlene had arrived. Even from across the room, she could smell her mother's perfume.

Kira finished closing up a box and moved it to the stack, ready to go out to the company van. Finally she turned to look at Charlene. Her mother. How could this woman have given birth to her? They were as different as . . . well, as different as the proverbial night and day. Today Charlene wore causal blue slacks with a cream-colored sweater. She looked almost serene and harmless—almost.

Kira didn't greet Charlene. Instead, she just crossed her arms and waited for her mother to get to the point of her visit.

"I had no idea you would be so busy." Charlene remained standing just inside the door.

"It's called work for a reason, Mother. I promised you five minutes. What is it you want?"

"Is it possible for you to take a break and go get some coffee?"

"Five minutes isn't enough time for that. You're wasting time." Kira pulled up her sleeve and glanced at her watch.

"Fine, have it your way. I just thought you would want to know what kind of a man you are mixed up with. Yes, I do care about you, whether you realize it or not."

"Yes, I'm sure," Kira said. "That must be why you tried to throw me out of my home."

"Oh, never mind that," her mother said. "This is much closer to your heart." She looked at Kira and smirked. "I did a bit of research on Mr. Grant Rutledge. If you must insist on raising a child—and a handicapped one at that—I think you should be a little more cautious about the men you let into your life. Especially ones who can't stand to be around their own child."

"What are you talking about?" Kira stared at Charlene in disbelief. Could Grant have a child? It couldn't be true. He loved children and wanted a family. He had made that very clear.

"Yes, Kira. I can see by your face you don't believe me. It's all here." Charlene pulled an envelope out of her jacket. "He left his fiancée when she was pregnant because he doesn't want children. Now she has the child, and he refuses to see it." Charlene leaned over and placed the envelope on the desk next to Kira. She said, "Grant took off when the going got tough. Is that really the type of man you want to have around your child?"

"I believe your time is up." Kira struggled to keep her voice as free of emotion as possible. She would not let Charlene know how the words were affecting her.

"Yes, of course. I'm so sorry, Kira. I hope we can see each other soon." Charlene took a hesitant step forward as if she intended to hug her daughter.

Kira raised both hands to stop her. "Just go. You have done enough. Goodbye."

Kira turned and walked to the back room. She didn't start shaking till the front door had clicked shut. She could hear her heart pounding in her ears. "It can't be possible," she thought. "Not Grant. I love him. It can't be the way she says."

"Kira? Are you okay?" Sarah came around the doorway.

"Yes. I'm all right." Kira sank down into a chair. "Did you hear what she said?"

"Yes. You don't believe her, do you? Kira, you know Grant. You have seen him with Jared. Grant loves children." Sarah grabbed Kira's hands. "You need to go talk to him about this. It is the only way you can get peace about it."

Kira turned back toward the computer so Sarah wouldn't see her tears. She said, "Right now, we have work to do. There are orders to put in the computer. I had yesterday off and I have things to catch up on here. I will talk to Grant later."

"But Kira—" Sarah began.

"Really, Sarah. I do appreciate your concern. But I need to handle this in my own way." Kira spent the rest of her hours on the computer catching up on paperwork —deliberately keeping her mind clear of thoughts of either Grant or Charlene. The phones were quiet. At two o'clock, she picked up the envelope that Charlene had left on the desk. Putting it in her tote, she said goodbye to Sarah and left to get Jared at school.

At home, she brewed some coffee and, after fixing a cup, made her way to the living room with the envelope. Jared was still in the kitchen, helping Barbara make gingerbread. She settled into the easy chair and sipped her coffee. For a long while, the envelope sat in her lap, unopened. She drank her coffee and just looked at it, wondering if it was worth opening. She replayed the months in which she had known Grant. Grant had really seemed to love Jared, and he had gone out of his way to learn about autism. He had asked questions about Jared's therapy and had even learned some signs. He had said time and time again how much he wanted a family of his own.

Kira struggled to hold off thoughts of Patrick and the disastrous marriage they had had, especially after Jared was born. Was the past reliving itself? Maybe it had been a mistake to try to trust a man again.

She sighed and picked up the envelope. She opened it slowly and pulled out the contents. Pictures and a report from a private investigator came out. She read it all carefully. Nausea rolled over her as she looked at the photos. She swallowed hard and closed her eyes. Was this what betrayal felt like? He had played her for a fool.

Did he truly not want to see his child? How could she talk to Grant about this?

Kira put all the contents back into the envelope and started to cry. What to do? If she didn't bring it up, she would always feel like he was hiding something from her. If she did, she ran the risk of losing him. She felt like her heart was breaking.

Chapter 20

Kira awoke to the ringing of the telephone. She glanced to the clock and saw that it was still Wednesday night. She had fallen asleep in the chair. In the kitchen Barb answered the phone, talking quietly. Jared was eating dinner, chatting up a storm. They must have decided to let her rest.

Kira sighed as she got up and started for the kitchen. She stopped in the doorway just as Barbara hung up the phone. "That was Grant. I didn't want to wake you."

"Oh. You should have wakened me for dinner." Kira sat at the table and watched Jared shovel spaghetti into his mouth.

"You looked pretty worn out. It must have been some day at work, especially after yesterday."

"Actually, Charlene stopped by. Apparently she felt the need to cause more turmoil."

"Did you tell Grant?"

"No, not yet." Kira got up and paced around the kitchen.

"What did Charlene say, Kira?" Barbara asked gently.

Kira quickly pointed toward Jared. "It isn't exactly the time to talk about it, Barb, and frankly, I'm not sure I'm up to going through it. Let's just say she seems to have a talent for finding dirt. This time she targeted Grant." Kira leaned against the counter and added, "Successfully."

Barbara crossed the room and laid a hand on Kira's arm, but she didn't ask any questions. Instead, she simply said, "Go take a hot bath and think this through. Grant wanted you to stop by the workshop at Marcus and Mary Lou's house. He said he has something important to show you. But given the state that you're in, I think it should wait."

"A bath sounds good. Thanks again, Barbara. It's been such a gift to have you back in my life." Kira reached over to gave Jared a kiss on the top of the head and started down the hall.

After a hot bath, Kira felt more relaxed, but she was still confused with regards to Grant and his child. She couldn't believe he would deny his own son. Yet, the information in the envelope appeared to be set in stone. The timeline was clear. He had broken off the engagement when his fiancée was pregnant. She had given birth to a boy, and Grant had had nothing to do with the child.

Kira had been ready to give her heart and soul to him. Now he was being painted as a man who ran from responsibility—very much like Patrick.

* * *

It was now or never. The sun was shining, but Kira felt like a cloud hung over her. She had tossed and turned all night. When she did sleep, she dreamed of Patrick and the car crash.

She dressed casually for work. She only worked a half day today and then planned to see Grant right afterward. Jared was out of school for Christmas break. Right now he was sleeping, but Barbara had agreed to keep an eye on him so she could speak with Grant after work.

She headed for the kitchen and grabbed some coffee. She leaned against the kitchen counter while she drank it, feeling her heart ache as she tried to imagine how the conversation with Grant would go. She couldn't imagine it going well. She wondered, "How do you talk to the man you love about a child he has been ignoring?"

She checked in on Jared and then headed off. She was the first to arrive at the shop. All of the orders had been unloaded, so Kira wandered around the store, rearranging scented candlesticks and doing other unnecessary tasks to keep her mind occupied.

By the time that Sarah arrived, Kira had taken a seat behind the desk, staring into space.

"Looks like a slow day today, Kira. Why don't you take it off?" Sarah said. "You worked hard yesterday."

Kira stood up and reached for her coat. "Actually, I'm going to take you up on that. Thanks. I need to see Grant and get some stuff straightened out."

"Go ahead." Sarah smiled. "I'll be in the shop all day in case any last-minute Christmas shoppers come in."

"Okay. I'll see you tomorrow." Kira quickly hugged Sarah and headed for her car. With her elbows on the steering wheel, she sat for a moment and gathered her thoughts. Then she headed to Marcus's workshop to see whatever it was that Grant had been working on so diligently.

* * *

As Kira pulled up next to Grant's Kia Sorento at Mary Lou and Marcus's house, she heard the sound of a radio coming from the workshop. She checked her tote for the hundredth time to make sure Charlene's envelope was there. She took a deep breath, braced herself, and opened the workshop door.

Grant stood there running his hands over a beautifully crafted wooden rocking horse. She saw the pride in his face as he eyed it to make sure it was perfectly smooth. She couldn't help but smile when he rocked it to check that the movement was seamless. He obviously had put a lot of time and effort into this. It was exactly what Jared had said he wanted from Santa.

None of this was making any sense. Kira thought, "Who is this man? Is this really the same person who walked away from his own child?"

"Hey," Kira said softly as she shut the workshop door.

"I didn't hear you come in. How long have you been there?"

"Not long. It's beautiful." Kira threw her tote to the bench and walked over to touch the rocking horse. The unfinished wood had been sanded to the texture of polished glass. The detail was in incredible. She rocked it gently, trying not to cry.

"Will he like it?" Grant asked.

"Oh, most definitely. How did you know he wanted one?"

"He mentioned it to me a while ago when we were talking about Santa."

"It's incredible, Grant. I had no idea you were doing this."

"I wanted to surprise you. Is it really okay?" Grant leaned against the workbench.

"Yes, of course it is. I'm just so thrown by this. I don't know what to say."

"Hey, you dropped something," Grant said. The envelope had fallen out of the tote, and Grant reached down and picked it up. The photos spilled onto the floor. "What is this?"

When Kira met Grant's eyes, his expression filled with rage. He threw the papers down on the workbench in disgust. "You hired a private investigator?"

"I did no such thing." Whatever she had imagined this meeting would be like, this wasn't it. He actually thought she'd been spying on him.

"How could you think that?" she asked.

"Well, you didn't return my call last night, and you certainly didn't bring this straight to my attention. It looks like you're acting more and more like your mother. Sneaking around, no one knows what you're really up to—"

"Grant . . . Charlene gave me those papers yesterday. I was in shock. I came over here today hoping you would have some answers."

"This is all news to me. But clearly you didn't trust me enough to come right out and ask me yourself."

"What do you want me to say, Grant? I'm here now, aren't I? I thought I knew you. Tell me it's not true. I look at the papers and see the words and photos in black-and-white, and logic tells me one thing. But then I look at you and our time together and my heart wants to tell me something else. It doesn't make sense to me."

"It doesn't make sense to me, either," Grant said. "Yes, I was engaged once. But Sophia was certainly not pregnant when we broke up—at least, not that I was ever aware of."

"Look at the report and the timeline, and see how it adds up."

"See how it adds up? I'll tell you what I see!" His voice was forceful now. "I see that once again you have jumped to conclusions that put me in a negative light. I see that you automatically assumed I'm just like Patrick—again. I see that you think I'm just another man who didn't want his child."

Grant took a step forward to close the gap between them. "After all we have been through together, I thought you knew me better than that."

Kira could see the pulse pounding along the side of Grant's neck. He said, "I thought we knew each other better, but I guess you don't really know me at all. I'm tired of being compared to Patrick!" He took a deep breath and looked her squarely in the eyes. "Be assured,

Kira. If this relationship is going to move even one single inch forward, then you need to realize that there is no more room for Patrick's ghost. You need to make a choice."

He picked the envelope back up. "I'm going to go make some phone calls. But you can trust me on this—and I mean it, Kira—it's either going to be me or him."

Chapter 21

Kira left the workshop in complete astonishment. She had never imagined that Grant might feel he played second to Patrick's ghost. She drove mindlessly for a while, trying to find a way to process the recent string of events. She suddenly realized she was at the site of Patrick's accident. Parking the car again, she walked to the edge of the cliff and sat on the new guardrail.

Memories flooded her heart once more. She had been so unhappy in the last few months of her marriage. Would it even be possible for her to recognize happiness again? *Was* she allowing Patrick's ghost to interfere with her new relationship? As she sat beside the cliff, she replayed the conversations between her and Grant. Each one seemed to end with her fear that he would end up reacting like Patrick. What a fool she had been.

Kira stood up. Grant was right. It was him or Patrick's ghost—and she didn't want Patrick's ghost. She wanted Grant. She was in love with Grant; he was the man she wanted in her life. How could she have been so stupid?

Kira squared her shoulders and started for her car. She had no idea how to fix this, but she had to somehow get through to Grant. She needed him in her life; Jared needed him in his life; and no matter what the story with the ex-fiancée turned out to be, she wasn't going to let him slip through her hands.

Kira drove home with new resolve. She would call Grant, and hopefully he would take her call. If he loved her like he said he did, he would forgive her and accept her support.

Upon arriving home, Kira tried calling Grant's apartment. There was no answer. His cell phone also seemed to be off. She then tried calling his parents' home. Mary Lou answered and told her that Grant had left an hour or so before. Where had he gone? Perplexed, she sat with the phone in her hand. Maybe he had gone to track down his former fiancée. Certainly Grant would want to know if she had a son or not. How could she have doubted that? She decided to give him his space and see what happened.

Barb came into the living room to join Kira. "How did it go with Grant today?"

"Not well," Kira said. She suddenly felt exhausted. "I didn't handle things well. He pretty much told me I need to choose between him or Patrick's ghost."

"Well, and there it is. Where does that put you?"

"He's right. I have been keeping him at arm's length. Oh, Barbara, I love him so much." Kira plucked a tissue from the box on the coffee table and wiped her eyes. "I think I blew it. Now, according to the papers Charlene gave me, he may have a child out there. I wouldn't be surprised if he has gone to see his ex-fiancée."

"And you're afraid of where it will go from there." Barbara watched her pointedly.

"Yes. I don't want to lose him."

"Well, you have opened your eyes then. You know what you want, and I think you know what you need to do. I have said it before, honey . . . follow your heart. I think you have finally let the barriers down." Barb came over and hugged her close. "It will be fine, just you wait and see."

"I hope so, Barb, I hope so."

* * *

Grant drove nearly eight hours to reach the small town listed in the detective's report. According to the highway signs, it was an easy commute from this town to New York City, which was probably what had drawn Sophia here in the first place. When he had last seen her in Texas, her modeling career had been on the verge of taking off. Her agent had been pushing for more magazine work, which would have required a move to a big city.

The closer he got to her address, the more furious he felt. It had been more than three years since they had broken off their engagement. Initially, he had been drawn in by her glamour. Looking back now, he realized that they'd had almost nothing in common at all.

The day they had split up, he knew it was time to get back to his roots. It was time to be more grounded and stop living in a dream. Sophia hadn't blinked an eye while he packed his things. In fact, she had sounded relieved. She had said she was going to pursue her modeling career and enjoy the freedom that came with being single. Marriage was definitely not in her future. She had mentioned some possible travel plans. Splitting up had clearly been the best choice for both of them.

Now Grant pulled in behind a BMW SUV. She must be doing well. The home itself was small, but real estate this close to the city must cost a small fortune anyway.

Taking the steps two at a time, he approached the door and rang the bell. As he waited impatiently, he heard movement inside. The door opened a few inches. A young girl of no more than twenty peeked out.

"Is Sophia home?" Grant asked. Could this be a roommate? She didn't have a younger sister.

"Yes, can I tell her who wants to see her?"

"Just tell her it's important. I'll wait here."

She shut the door and he heard her talking quietly to someone inside. The curtain pulled back slightly as someone looked out to the porch. After a moment, the door opened and Sophia stepped outside. "What are you doing here, Grant?"

"Sophia. Well, that is quite a welcome. Aren't you glad to see me? I've come a long way."

"I don't know about glad, but I'm certainly surprised. How did you find me?"

"A private detective, as a matter of fact. And not even my own. But he says you've been keeping a secret from me."

The color drained from Sophia's face as Grant leaned on the porch railing and crossed his arms.

"I have no idea what you're talking about," she said.

"No? I think you do. How's our son?"

"Our son." Sophia's voice trembled. "How did you . . ."

"Like I said. Someone told me your secret. I want to know why I'm the last one to hear. You knew how I felt about a family, Sophia. Where is he? What's his name?"

Sophia put out a hand and grabbed the porch railing as if she might fall. Then she took a deep breath and looked at Grant. "His name is Kyle."

"So we do have a son!" Grant stared at her in disbelief. "You and I have a son together, and you kept me out of his life all this time?"

"Grant, you have to understand . . ."

"What?" Grant crossed the space between them and yanked her arm from the railing. "What is it you want me to understand? For the past two and half years you kept my son from me and I'm supposed to understand?"

"Okay. I get that you're upset." Sophia backed up against the door. "It's complicated. "Come inside. Just please try to stay calm and I will try to explain."

"Stay calm?"

"Grant, please. I will let you see him. But let's not upset Daphne."

"Daphne?"

"She's the au pair." Sophia led the way into the house.

Grant trailed behind her. "You have an au pair? Why aren't you taking care of Kyle yourself?"

"I'm modeling. I can't drag him along with me. You can't just have a toddler running around during a photo shoot. You're lucky you caught me today. I'm usually out of town."

Grant grabbed her arm again to stop her. "Do you hear yourself? You're usually out of town? Are you involved in Kyle's life at all? Or are you just too wrapped up in your own life, Sophia?"

"Grant, what do you know about children?"

"Apparently more than you. They need love, and they need your time. You can't just dump them with an au pair." He ran his fingers through his hair in disgust.

Sophia glared at Grant. "I'm his mother, Grant. I can do as I see fit with him."

"Don't be so sure of yourself. I will tell you this: I will fight you for him.."

"You can't just take him from me." Sophia stopped and faced him.

"Take him from you? Or from the au pair? Do you feed him, change him, and spend time with him yourself? Or do you just write a big fat check each month to the hired help and call yourself the mother?"

Grant was steaming by now. "Take me to my son, Sophia. I have gone long enough without seeing him."

It seemed that one look at Grant's face was enough to stop any refusals on Sophia's part. She led him further down the hallway to a small playroom.

Grant shoved past her as soon as he saw the little boy, who was playing on the floor, surrounded by toys. Grant stopped in his tracks. Kyle's wavy dark hair reminded him of baby pictures of himself. Grant smiled as Kyle began to sing the alphabet song to his teddy bear. He seemed like a happy child.

Grant went over and sat on the floor in front of Kyle. He was immediately overcome by a surge of love for the child. He took a deep breath and began to play with the boy, following Kyle's lead.

After a few moments, Grant glanced up to look at Sophia, who was watching from the side of the room without much apparent interest. He turned back to Kyle.

"I have to go now, Kyle, but I'll see you again soon. It's been really fun to play with you."

The little boy waved goodbye and then reached for his bear again.

Grant motioned for Sophia to follow him back out into the hall. "I'm going to find a place in town to stay for a few days. You will hear from my lawyer, Sophia. I will be filing for custody of my son." He headed to the door.

"You can't!" Sophia followed.

Grant turned to face her. "You have kept my son from me for almost three years. You've hired someone else to take care of him instead of doing it yourself. I want to take care of my son myself. See you in court."

From his car, he glanced to the house to see Sophia looking out. For the first time, Grant allowed himself to imagine his future as Kyle's father. He smiled as his thoughts quickly moved from the little boy to Kira. She would be the perfect mother for his son. But then he frowned again. So many questions still needed an answer. Would she ever find it in herself to let go of Patrick? And could they all move forward as a family with *two* sons—Jared and Kyle?

Grant's mind was reeling as he drove back toward the town center to find a place to stay. He wished he could share his excitement and trepidation with Kira, but he had asked her to make a choice. Now he needed to wait to see what her decision would be.

Chapter 22

Grant had just booked a hotel room when his cell phone rang. Answering, he was stunned by the voice at the other end.

"Hello?"

"Grant. It's me, Sophia."

"What do you want, Sophia?" Looking back, he remembered that she had always been manipulative, never hesitating to bend the truth to get whatever she had wanted. Well, now his son was involved. He didn't have the time or the patience for any more of her games.

"I thought we could get together and talk. How about dinner tomorrow night? All three of us. Kyle, you, and me."

"Where?"

"You could come back to the house. Might be easier for Kyle."

"So now you're thinking of Kyle first?" He could hear the bitterness creep into his voice. "Fine. I will be there at six."

Grant clicked the phone shut and wondered what she was up to. It had been less than an hour since he had threatened her with a custody suit. Was she worried about bad publicity? One thing he knew for sure: her career would always come first.

* * *

The next evening, Grant rang Sophia's doorbell again. He had spent the day on his laptop doing research for the development on the coast. He had decided to postpone the discussion with a custody lawyer until he had more information from Sophia. On the ride over, he had run through several possible scenarios for this meeting in his mind. He didn't believe Sophia had Kyle's best interests at heart. So what did she really want now?

The door opened abruptly. Grant surveyed the living room as he stepped inside. Kyle was playing on the floor with blocks. Once again, a rush of love took Grant by surprise as he watched Kyle. His heart would break if he didn't find a way to have his son with him permanently.

From the look of Sophia's designer outfit, which included a slim black skirt that barely covered the top of her thighs, he doubted that she had been on the floor playing with Kyle. Daphne, the au pair, was nowhere in sight.

Grant lowered himself to sit beside the little boy. Kyle immediately crawled into his lap and handed him a toy truck. His son's smile widened as Grant made motor noises and pushed the truck across the rug. Kyle put his head on his father's shoulder, and Grant held him tight. Then he looked up at Sophia.

"So Kyle is joining us for dinner tonight?"

"Of course he is. What did you expect?" Sophia's voice was smooth and showed no hesitation. She had always been a good actress. He wondered if her confidence was just a bluff.

He frowned. "So what is it you really wanted, Sophia?"

"Nothing. Thought you might like to spend some time with your son, that's all." She started for the kitchen. "I'm going to check on dinner. It should be just about ready."

"I'm sure the au pair did a great job."

Sophia scowled and then stormed into the kitchen. Grant turned and smiled at Kyle. "How about I roll you the ball?"

A few minutes later, Grant picked up his son and made his way to the kitchen.

"Is dinner ready? Kyle must be hungry." Grant headed for the high chair and placed Kyle in it.

"Yes. Let me just put things on the table. Do you want to get Kyle's plate ready?" Sophia kept her back to Grant as she talked.

"I can do that. You probably don't know how."

Sophia turned around quickly. "You don't like me very much anymore, do you?"

"You've kept me from my own son for almost three years, Sophia. How am I supposed to feel?"

Grant sat beside Kyle, who was banging his spoon on the tray. "Let's find a bib for you, buddy. Sophia, do you have a bib?"

Sophia blushed as she started rifling through drawers. "I'm sure there must be one here somewhere . . ."

Sophia never did find a bib, so Grant improvised with a paper towel. He helped Kyle with his dinner, washed the boy's hands at the sink, and then returned him to his high chair.

"Didn't you like the chicken?" Sophia asked. She pointed to Grant's plate, which was still half full.

"It was fine. I just thought I should take care of Kyle —something I have yet to see you do." Grant glared at her.

"I do take care of him. Sometimes. I just thought you'd want to do it tonight."

He doubted her motivation. "How often is 'sometimes,' really?"

When she simply shrugged, he asked, " Why on earth didn't you just tell me we had a child?"

Instead of answering, she quickly asked, "How did you find out? Was there really a detective involved?"

"There was, but not mine. I learned about Kyle from someone who had my best interests at heart." Grant felt a stab of guilt as he thought of the way he had argued with Kira when he found the papers. He had acted like a fool.

"Was it someone who knew both of us?" Her eyes widened as if she was afraid.

"Look, Sophia. Let's just cut to the chase here. It was a friend of mine. The word isn't going to spread any further. Are you worried about what a custody battle might do for your career?"

She suddenly straightened her posture and tugged at the hem of her skirt. "No, not at all. I'm quite confident it won't change a thing."

Suddenly Kyle pushed his plate off the high chair. Sophia reached out and grabbed it just before it went over the edge.

"Good reflexes," Grant said. "Maybe you have some of a mother's instinct after all."

Grant stood up and took Kyle from the high chair. The little boy settled into Grant's lap and put his head on his shoulder.

"What time does he usually go to bed?" Grant asked.

"Oh, probably anytime now." Sophia waved her hand.

"Should you be getting him ready?"

"Well, I suppose. But would you like to put him to bed? Then I can clean up the kitchen." She picked up Grant's plate and added, "I think at night he gets a diaper change."

Grant changed Kyle's diaper and found some pajamas in a drawer near the crib. He hummed as he helped Kyle with the zipper. It all felt so natural.

He rocked Kyle until he was asleep and then placed him in the crib. He gently rubbed the little boy's back and gazed at him in amazement. This little boy was his flesh and blood. His son. Sighing, he turned to leave the nursery and face Sophia's next set of moves.

For a brief moment, Grant leaned against the doorframe of the living room and simply watched Sophia, who was sitting on the couch. He hesitated when she looked up at him and patted the cushion next to her.

"Is he off to sleep?" she asked.

"Yes, nice and easy." He sat beside her, leaving a wide space between them. "What's this all about, Sophia? Did you think about what I said yesterday? Are you going to let me have custody of my son?"

"I did." She hesitated and then met his gaze. "I think we can work something out."

He carefully hid his disdain as she slid a hand up his

arm. Then she said, "Things used to be so good between us."

"What kind of memories do you have?" He pulled his arm away. "We fought constantly, Sophia."

"In the end, yes, but we had good times too. We were engaged."

"Was it really love, though, or just the idea of it?" Grant asked. He realized he was thinking aloud.

Sophia pulled his arm back and snuggled closer. She smiled. "I loved you, Grant."

"Maybe."

Suddenly, she wrapped her arms around his neck and kissed his lips.

Grant pushed her away. "What was that?"

"I want to try again. I want us to try for Kyle's sake."

"You're serious?" Grant edged out of her grasp and stood up.

Sophia stood too, holding on to his arm. "Are you telling me you feel nothing?"

Grant grabbed both of her arms. "That's right. I feel nothing, Sophia, and I want nothing to do with you. *I want my son.* Can I make that any clearer?"

The phone rang, interrupting them. Grant grabbed his coat. "Go ahead and answer that. I'll be at my hotel. Think about what I've said, and call me when you're ready to talk seriously."

Chapter 23

Back at the hotel, Grant began to plan for his new life with Kyle. His apartment was small, but it would do for a while. There was plenty of space for a child.

He had given Sophia a lot to think about. He would wait one more day before calling the lawyer. Grant had no doubt that Sophia was so concerned with her career, she wouldn't want lawyers involved.

He was furious with the way she ignored Kyle. She was no mother to him. From what he had seen, the au pair must be in charge nearly 24/7.

Grant moved to the desk and grabbed a pad of paper with the hotel's logo, intending to make a list of what he needed for a toddler. As he looked for a pen, however, he realized that he had no idea where to even start. Kira would know, but his pride kept him from calling her. His mom would know. He sighed. He probably ought to break this news to his parents sooner than later.

As he called the Rutledge home, his mind was filled with thoughts of Kyle. He wondered what the little boy's first few years had been like.

When Mary Lou picked up the phone and heard his voice, she said, "Grant! Finally! Where on earth are you? Kira called the other day looking for you. She sounded upset."

"I had to go away for a few days. In fact, I'm still away. What did she want?"

"She didn't say, and I didn't ask. What's going on with you two?"

"Actually, I need to talk to you and Dad. Can you put him on the other line?"

"This sounds serious," Mary Lou said. Grant could hear her sigh. "I think he's out in the workshop. Hold on just a moment and I'll go get him."

Grant watched the holiday traffic streaming past the hotel window as he waited for his parents to get on the line. Finally he heard Marcus pick up the second receiver.

"We're listening," Marcus said.

"Kira and I had a fight because, well . . . apparently her mother hired a private investigator to investigate me."

"What on earth for?" Marcus exclaimed.

"I have no idea why, but he came up with some interesting stuff."

"What stuff?" Mary Lou asked.

"Remember the relationship I had while I was still in Texas?" Grant took a deep breath and rubbed his hand across the back of his neck, which was stiff with tension. "Her name was Sophia."

"Yes." His parents answered in unison.

"Evidently, when we broke off our engagement, she was pregnant."

Grant could hear his mother gasp on the other end of the line. "Pregnant! Did she have the baby?"

Marcus cut in. "Is it definitely yours?"

"Yes, she had the baby, and I would also say yes to him being mine, given the timeline and the fact that he looks like me."

"Why didn't she tell you?" his father demanded.

"I don't know. She probably just wanted to focus on her career without having to answer to me. I'm in New York, which is where she lives now. I went to see her tonight. Her modeling career has really taken off. But as far as I can tell, she constantly dumps the little boy with Daphne, his au pair."

"That's not okay!" In his mind, Grant could picture Mary Lou shaking her head. "A child needs at least one parent to be properly engaged in his life. What are you going to do about all this?"

"I want to raise my son."

"Good for you." Marcus's voice broke a little as he added, "We're behind you."

"I'm proud of you," Mary Lou cut in. "Tell us what you need from us." Then she laughed as if the news had just started to sink in. "A grandchild! What's his name? I can't wait to see him."

"It's Kyle. And thanks, Mom and Dad."

After a lengthy discussion about Grant's intentions, they hung up. Hope filled him again. Marcus and Mary Lou had been supportive and were clearly quite excited to meet their grandson.

Grant felt a twang of guilt for not calling Kira, but he was determined to hold fast. He would wait for her to call him. He needed to know she was committed to this relationship and that she could leave the past behind. But he hoped she'd call sooner than later. He really wanted to share this news with her.

* * *

Grant awoke the next morning full of energy. He ordered breakfast from room service and began another list of things to buy for Kyle. As he was making a list of furniture to turn his spare room into a nursery, the phone rang.

"Hello?"

"Can we meet?" The silky, distinct voice of Sophia came across the line.

"Have you come to your senses?" Grant asked.

"I want to talk. There is so much to explain. Please, Grant."

"Fine. I'll meet you at the coffee shop in the center of town in an hour." Grant hung up, giving Sophia no room for argument.

As he set the phone back in his pocket, Grant wondered if she had come to her senses. She needed to admit once and for all that her career simply left no room for Kyle in her life—and that he would be better off in Grant's care.

He left, hoping to beat her to the coffee shop. Maybe he could take Kyle home to Maine in time for Christmas.

At the coffee shop, Grant found a booth in the back and ordered a decaf coffee with extra cream. Then he waited.

As he sipped his coffee, he was determined to make sure they came to an arrangement today. He stood as she approached. Today she was wearing a navy tweed topcoat and form-fitting black leggings.

"Thanks for meeting me, Grant." Sophia slid into the booth.

"Good morning," he said. "Why don't you go head and order. Then I would like to get this resolved." Softening his tone, he added, "As I am sure you would. I know we both want what's best for Kyle here."

Sophia ordered a black coffee and removed her scarf, which looked like fur. The she said, "I'm not sure where to begin."

"How about at the beginning?" Grant said. "Why didn't you call me when you found out you were pregnant?"

She sighed. "I was in shock. I didn't want to have the baby at first, but then my agent said I could do some photo shoots for pregnancy magazines." Sophia played with her drink. "After he was born I contemplated putting him up for adoption, but I had already placed your name on the birth certificate. I had a cesarean section, and my mind was pretty cloudy. Once your name was on the birth certificate, I couldn't arrange an adoption without getting your signature."

"My God, Sophia," Grant said. "Didn't it ever occur to you that I'd want him?"

She shrugged. "I guess. But I knew you'd have all sorts of lofty ideas about how he should be raised. It just seemed easier to try to manage things on my own."

Grant paused for a long moment to pull his anger back under control. Finally he said, "So what are your plans now?"

"Well, that's why I wanted to meet. Yesterday I received a long-term job offer to model in Paris. It is a chance of a lifetime for me." Sophia's voice came alive now.

"You're not taking Kyle." Grant's voice was adamant.

"Of course not. The Paris lifestyle is no place for a child!"

"I guess I'm back to my original question then—what exactly are your plans?" Grant was starting to feel hopeful, but he deliberately tried to keep his demeanor cool.

"Well, I don't really want to drag lawyers—or newspapers—into this. Daphne has been talking about going back to college anyway. Maybe the best place for Kyle would be with you right now." Sophia gave him the innocent-seeming smile that used to melt his heart. But he knew better than to fall for it now.

"Immediately? Listen, Sophia, when he comes with me, you will need to sign papers giving me full custody. There will be no chance that someday you will decide you want him back. You will not do that to him." Grant sat back in the booth. Hope soared through his heart. He was confident she would agree.

"Are you saying I can't ever see him?" The corners of her mouth turned down as if she was pretending to pout.

"You can see him upon agreement, but I will continue with full custody. I will have my lawyers draw up the papers." Grant clenched his fits and added, "It will be kept very quiet. You won't have to worry about your career. But I want Kyle immediately."

He stood up and grabbed his keys. "When are you leaving for Paris?"

"Next week."

"Fine. Why don't I follow you back to your place and help you pack up some of Kyle's things. Then he can come home with me today."

"The au pair may want a chance to say goodbye."

"The au pair? How sad is that. What about you, Sophia?"

Sophia grabbed her purse and avoided his gaze. She said, "You just don't understand, Grant. I need to work on my career. This call came in last night as you were leaving."

"I understand everything," he thought grimly. But all he said to Sophia was, "Let's go. I'm anxious to be with my son."

Chapter 24

Grant pulled into Sophia's driveway right behind her. He wasn't taking a chance she'd change her mind.

He reminded himself to try to hide his irritation at her lack of feelings for Kyle. He took a deep breath to slow his racing heart, which he could hear pounding in his ears. Setting out on this new path with his son was both exciting and nerve-wracking all that the same time. There could be tough days ahead. How would the little guy react to moving in with a total stranger?

Grant got out of the Sorento, grabbed some empty shopping bags from the back seat, and followed Sophia into the house. She walked into the kitchen and picked up a note.

"Daphne took him to the park," she said. "That should give us a chance to pack his things."

Grant moved aside as Sophia pushed past and headed for the nursery, where she started opening closet doors. She pulled out a large duffle bag, opened some drawers, and began throwing in Kyle's clothes.

Grant held up one of the empty shopping bags. "What are his favorite toys?" he asked.

"I don't know. You'd have to ask the au pair."

"Never mind. I'll just make my best guess and then check when she returns."

Grant finished packing up toys, clothes, and anything else he thought he would need. Sophia left to take a phone call, leaving him alone. He wandered around the room. He stopped at the crib and ran his hand over the railing. He pictured his son lying there as a newborn. His heart tugged as he imagined Kyle pulling himself up on the rails for the first time.

"Did you get everything? Sophia just filled me in on what is going on."

It was Daphne. She was holding Kyle, who looked like he could use a nap.

"I think so. Is there anything special he sleeps with?"

"He won't sleep unless he has his Pooh bear. Did you pack that?" She went to the crib.

"Yes. Do you think he will transition to a toddler bed now if it has a rail?"

"He should do okay. He sleeps well." Her voice suddenly broke and she wiped away a tear. "Sorry about that. I'm not sure why I'm getting so emotional. I was going to sign up for school anyway. But it still feels hard." She kissed the top of Kyle's head. "He's really a sweet little boy."

Grant smiled at her. "It seems like you've done a great job. Is there anything else I should know?"

"Well, he chokes sometimes on food if the pieces are too big. Don't give him hot dogs yet. He doesn't like a lot of veggies, but he loves fruit." Daphne wiped away another tear. "Don't worry. I'll be fine, and he'll be fine with you. You obviously care for him. He never saw her, you know."

"I figured as much," Grant said. "I just want what's best for him."

"I'll say goodbye to him while you put this stuff in your car. Here are my keys. Take his car seat from my car."

Grant loaded up the SUV and buckled in the car seat.

Daphne brought Kyle out of the house. As Grant handed back her keys, she said, "Sophia's still on the phone. But she paused for a minute and said I should tell you to just get going."

Grant reached for the little boy. "Hi, Kyle."

Kyle leaned into Grant's shoulder without reservation. Grant said softly, "Ready to go with Dad?" Speaking those words felt incredible.

Kyle lifted his head and leaned back to study Grant somberly. Then his expression shifted and he gave Daphne a cheerful wave. Grant took a deep breath as he strapped the little boy in the car seat. For the first time all morning, he gave a huge sigh of relief. It was done. His son was with him. The journey was just beginning. He wasn't sure where it might lead, but he was ready.

* * *

Kyle slept most of the way back to Maine. Right before it got dark, Grant stopped at a fast food place with an indoor playground so the toddler could run off some steam. But once they were back in the car and he had a dry diaper, he promptly fell back asleep.

When they finally arrived home, Grant slung the duffel bag over one shoulder and carried Kyle in his other arm. He thought, "How on earth am I supposed to get all this in the house without leaving Kyle alone? How do single parents do this?"

He made another trip out to the car with Kyle. This time, he brought the playpen in. He set it up in his living room and placed the boy down with a few toys. Then he sprinted back and forth between the apartment and the

SUV, bringing in the last armload of his son's belongings. Kyle was playing contentedly with his toys, so Grant started putting his clothes away in the guestroom. As he moved sheets and towels out of the bureau to make room for Kyle's little outfits, he enjoyed listening to his son's laughter as he played in the other room.

The sound of sudden crying brought Grant running. However, when he arrived in the living room, Kyle was simply standing at the side of the playpen. The little boy saw him and laughed.

"Oh, playing games with Dad, huh?" Grant joined in the laughter and picked his son up. "How about a snack before bedtime?"

Grant rummaged through his cabinets and found a box of cheese-flavored crackers. Afterwards he found that bathing a toddler was not an easy task.

Thirty minutes later, a soaking wet Grant settled Kyle down in front of the television. Flipping through the channels, he found one that seemed to be showing PBS programs for children around the clock. Then he collapsed on the couch next to Kyle. The past few days had been exhausting—but totally worth it. Kyle snuggled close with his Pooh bear clutched to his chest. Grant hugged him, amazed at the scent of his own shampoo in this little guy's hair. Then Grant nestled Kyle into some blankets, which he had placed across cushions on the floor. He dug through a closet, found his old sleeping bag, and set it up on the floor beside his son. They could shop for a toddler bed in the morning.

As Grant rubbed Kyle's back, he found himself humming a tune his mom had always hummed to him as a child. Then, as Kyle drifted off to sleep, he wondered what Kira was doing.

Chapter 25

Grant awoke stiff and sore. It had been a long night. Although Kyle had fallen asleep quickly, he had been up most of the night after that. Grant had spent those hours intermittently pacing the floor and rocking the little boy, developing a new respect for his mother and all those sleepless nights she had spent with him and his brothers. Somewhere close to dawn, Kyle had finally fallen asleep, but now those final hours in the sleeping bag on the floor were catching up with him.

He had been right to expect a tough transition between households. Making his way to the kitchen to brew some coffee, Grant hoped Kyle would at least nap this afternoon.

While the coffee brewed, Grant's mind wandered again to Kira. It had been a couple of days and he still hadn't heard from her. His heart ached at the thought of losing her. But he had made his case very clear. The only thing left to do was to give her time to think this through.

Pouring coffee, Grant inhaled the rich aroma. Just the smell of it gave his brain the boost he needed. The first sip was heaven. Again he wondered how single parents managed. He was determined to make a go of this, but he needed to get organized. He had less than a week to do some Christmas shopping for Kyle. Maybe next year he could make a second rocking horse.

First things first, though. Today Kyle needed to meet his grandparents. Grant smiled. Yup, Mom and Dad would be beside themselves.

In the other room, Kyle stirred. Grant headed toward the living room and braced himself for the start of day with a toddler.

"Hey, Kyle, Daddy's here." His son was lying on his side, holding his Pooh bear and looking around.

Upon seeing Grant, Kyle broke out in a huge smile. "Da da."

"Yup, Da da." The words brought tears to Grant's eyes. "Let's get you changed." He carried Kyle into his new room, picked out an outfit, and grabbed a fresh diaper. Then he returned to the cushions on the floor and started the process of dressing Kyle.

Kyle lay still, watching Grant.

"You're a good boy. Giving Dad a break, huh?" Grant talked with him as he dressed him. He was slow but he would get faster at it. "All set. Got Pooh bear?"

Kyle grabbed his bear. "Juice."

"Yup, let's get some juice, and cereal." Grant picked Kyle up again and headed toward the kitchen. He would need to add a highchair or booster seat to his shopping list.

After breakfast, Grant cleaned up the dishes and helped Kyle brush his teeth with the little green toothbrush Daphne had packed for him.

"Ready to go meet Nana and Papa?" Grant asked.

Driving to the Rutledge home, Grant talked about his parents. He was drawn back to his own childhood as he reminisced about building the tree house with his dad.

Then his thoughts drifted from the tree house to Jared and Kira. For a moment, he felt like a sledgehammer had hit him in the stomach. Remembering the fun he had had with Jared simply brought back the loneliness of Kira being gone.

He needed to snap out of this. "Come on, Kyle." Grant unbuckled the little boy from the car seat and started for the house.

Before they were halfway up the path, the door flung open and out ran Mary Lou and Marcus. "It's about time you got here. We've been waiting for hours!" Mary Lou said. "I've got pancakes made."

Grant smiled. "I should have known. Good morning, Mom and Dad. This is Kyle."

"Will you come to Nana, Kyle?" Mary Lou put her arms out and Kyle immediately leaned toward her with a big grin.

"Juice?"

"Nana will get you some juice. Come on inside. Do you want a pancake too?" Mary Lou was clearly in her glory as she whisked Kyle inside.

Marcus stood beside Grant and laughed. "You realize you won't see that boy again until it's time to leave, son. Your mother has wanted to be a grandmother for quite a while. She has already gone shopping, and the house is full of toys. She has been up for hours waiting for you to get here. I had to stop her from calling you an hour ago."

"It's okay, Dad. I could use the help this morning. I really appreciate Mom more than ever after the long night we had. I don't know how she stayed up all night with us when we were kids and then still functioned all day."

Marcus chuckled. "New appreciation for a lot of things when you become a father. How about some coffee?"

"Sounds good." They started inside.

"Have you talked to Kira?"

"No!" Marcus looked surprised to hear the sharpness in Grant's voice. Grant took a deep breath. "Sorry. A bit of a sore subject, I guess." He picked up the mugs of coffee Mary Lou had poured for them.

"If it bothers you that you haven't heard from her, why not just call her?" Mary Lou said. She was helping Kyle with his pancake and did not look up.

Grant smiled at the mess Kyle was making. "I'm not calling her. I asked that she think about some things. I assume she will call when she's done thinking."

Mary Lou raised her eyebrows at Marcus and then looked directly at Grant. "Sounds like you have a bit of Rutledge blood in you. And I don't mean that as a compliment."

"What does that mean?" Grant walked over to sit at the table.

"It means you're as stubborn as your father."

"Stubborn?"

Mary Lou cleaned up Kyle with a damp cloth. She put him on the floor beside a pile of new toys and then sat down across from Grant. "Yes, stubborn, Grant. It's written all over your face how much you miss her. Can you honestly say you don't want to just pick up that phone and share everything about Kyle with her?"

"Well, okay. Of course, I want to tell her about Kyle. . . but—"

"But what?"

"Mary Lou, don't push the boy." Marcus broke in. "He's got a lot on his plate right now." "Dad, it's okay. I know what she's saying." Grant looked down at Kyle and was silent for a moment. "He is a miracle. I didn't expect to be having a child in my life right now, much less a two-year-old. And yes, it rips me in half that Kira's not beside me right now so I can share it with her. All I think about is her. I do want to pick up the phone and talk to her, tell her every little thing he has done, and ask questions because I know she would know the right thing to do. She is such a good mother."

"Then call her."

"I can't. I gave her an ultimatum, Mom. Yes, I was a fool. Don't you think I know that? I'm almost thirty and probably just blew the best thing I have ever had in my life." Grant closed his eyes.

"An ultimatum?" Marcus spoke up again. "What do you mean?"

"I told her there was no room for Patrick's ghost in our relationship. It was him or me. And then I walked out. It was the day she told me what Charlene had found out about Kyle."

Grant saw Mary Lou and Marcus exchange glances as he began to pace the kitchen. He ran his fingers through his wavy hair. How could he have done this? He went over the scene again and again in his head. He should have handled it differently. Kira had probably been scared out of her mind when had she come to see him that day, afraid of how he would handle it. And what had he done? Run out on her.

"So what are you going to do?" Mary Lou asked.

"I honestly don't know. I love her. I keep hoping she'll call. I miss her and Jared so much."

"What's really stopping you, except your pride?" Mary Lou looked at him. "Grant, only you can decide what you need—and want—to do. My only advice is to listen to your heart."

"She's right." Marcus sat back in his chair now. "You know I don't usually say too much to you about your romantic life." He smiled then and added, "I usually let your mother do the meddling."

"Marcus!"

Marcus and Grant laughed. "But I will say this. We both love Kira and Jared like family. Kira has struggled for many years. When you came home after your breakup with Sophia, you had all the family support you needed to get rooted again. Who did Kira have all these years? Barbara, but no one else. Seems to me she is just getting settled again, but suddenly you're throwing ultimatums around. People don't change as quickly as we want sometimes. At times we need patience. And other times we're too stubborn for our own good."

He smiled again and turned to Mary Lou. "And I include myself in that."

"All good advice," Grant said. "I promise to think about it."

"Good. And now we have a grandson to enjoy. You look tired. Why don't you go lay down for a while?" Mary Lou suggested.

"Actually, if you don't mind watching Kyle, I would like to go finish up Jared's rocking horse."

"Mind watching my grandson? Go. Get out of here." Mary Lou shooed him out of the kitchen.

Grant bent and kissed Kyle. "Have fun with Nana and Papa."

Chapter 26

Kira awoke on Christmas Eve with mixed feelings. It had been a week since she had talked to Grant. She had put off going to see him for long enough. She had tried to call him a couple of times, but had only received his answering machine. She hadn't bothered to leave a message. She needed to talk to him in person. With Christmas fast approaching, she wanted all this behind her. All week long, Jared had kept asking her if Grant would be coming over on Christmas because he wanted to give him a present.

It was time to clear the air. Why had she waited so long? Why hadn't he called? She knew the answer. He had told her she needed to make a decision. She had made it a week ago, but ever since then she had allowed excuses to prevent her from acting on it.

She heard Jared running around in the living room, looking at the wrapped presents under the tree, trying to guess what they were. He was going to crash tonight if he kept this up. Sighing, she got out of bed. It would be a long day. She hoped she had judged Grant's reaction correctly. She had become quite used to the help Grant gave her. She wondered what had become of his search for his ex-fiancée and their son.

After dressing in jeans and a chunky sweater, Kira joined Jared in the living room. "You need to stop counting presents. Nothing has changed, Jared." She laughed as she sank into the easy chair.

"Do you think Santa will bring me a rocking horse?" Jared climbed into her lap.

"I don't know. He has to deliver to a lot of kids. You will just have to wait and see. If he doesn't, you need to be thankful for what he does bring you." Her heart ached for Grant. She had no idea if Grant would bring the rocking horse now or not. She had a backup present for Jared, but she didn't want to disappoint him.

"I know. I really want a rocking horse. Santa makes them right there in his workshop." Jared moved constantly in his excitement.

"Yes, I know. Did you want to watch a movie this morning? Maybe it will help you settle down a bit. How about a Christmas movie?"

"Okay." Jared ran off to pick out one of his favorites while Kira went to pour coffee.

Hearing the television start, Kira picked up the phone and dialed Grant's number once again. After several rings, the deep voice she had been longing to hear came across the line. "Hello?"

"Grant. It's Kira."

"Hi. How are you?" Kira's stomach clenched. She wasn't able to read Grant's mood with so few words.

"I'm good. You?" Kira continued the small talk, wondering how to bring the conversation around to what they really needed to discuss.

"Good, busy. You know how it is this time of year. What's going on?"

"We need to talk. I've been trying to call you this past week. I know I haven't left messages, but we really should talk in person." She paced around the kitchen, awaiting his reaction.

"We do have a lot to talk about. A lot has happened in a week."

Kira wondered if that was an indication of what was to come. Did that mean he no longer wanted anything to do with her? What if he'd gotten back together with Sophia?

She asked, "Are you busy now? Do you want to meet somewhere, or could you come over?"

"Is Jared home?"

"Yes."

"Great. I'll come over," Grant said.

"Okay. I'll see you in a little bit."

"Kira, just so you know. I have my son with me."

"Oh, that's wonderful, Grant. For the holiday?" Kira stopped pacing.

"It's a long story. Like I said, there's a lot to talk about. We'll both be there in a little bit." Grant hung up with a soft click.

As Kira put down the phone, her mind felt like a whirlwind. Obviously this was the reason she hasn't been able to get hold of Grant all week. She thought again, "Is Sophia back in the picture? What is going on?" She dropped into the kitchen chair as her mind worked overtime, racing with the possibilities. Her heart felt like there was a vise around it. She didn't want to lose him. She couldn't.

* * *

The sound of Kira's voice stirred emotions that Grant had never felt before. He missed her, of that he was sure. A week had gone by, and he had feared she wouldn't bother to call at all. Now he knew that she had called, but she hadn't left any messages. What had she wanted to say?

Looking around the apartment, he realized he hadn't gotten a Christmas tree. He had finished shopping, bought presents, and even wrapped them. But where did he think he would put them for Kyle to open on Christmas Day?

Grant shook his head. Kira would have thought of all of these details. He wondered how she would feel when she realized that he had Kyle permanently. He sighed. He supposed he would find out soon enough.

"Kyle, let's find your coat." Grant picked up some of the toys strewn about the living room.

"'Bye?" Kyle said.

"Yes, we're going 'bye." Grant laughed and watched his son run as fast as his chubby toddler legs could take him to get his coat. He was amazed at how much love he felt for this little boy after just a short week.

As Grant buckled Kyle into his car seat, he talked about Jared and Kira and where they were going. As they drove, Grant wondered again how Kira would react. Knowing Kira, she would probably fall in love with Kyle. She was a good mother; she would accept Kyle. Jared, on the other hand, might have trouble with change, especially around the holiday season. Still, Grant hoped for the best.

As he pulled into the driveway, he saw that the house was aglow with Christmas decorations. Very nice. Kira had gone all out this year. She had been thrilled that Grant had been willing to help her hang lights outside. Jared had loved it. Now Grant pointed them out to Kyle, who squealed with delight.

Grant opened the car door and heard Jared yell, "Grant's here!" The little boy dashed back into the house as if to further announce Grant's arrival. Well, Jared was happy to see him, at least. He hoped the same would be true for Kira. He unbuckled Kyle, picked him up, and started for the door. It flung open again and Jared rushed to him. Grant bent down and scooped him up in his free arm.

"Hi, Jared."

"Grant. Where've you been?" Jared flung his arms around his neck. "Who's this?"

"This is Kyle, my son."

"Hi, Kyle," Jared said.

Kyle watched Jared and laid his head on Grant's shoulder.

"He's a little shy because he doesn't know you yet. He's only two." Grant put Jared down. "Let's go in before all the heat comes out."

Grant walked into the house and caught his breath. Kira was standing there watching him. She was wearing skinny jeans and a sky blue chunky sweater. She appeared nervous, but she lit up at the sight of him.

"Hey, you," Kira said softly as she walked over.

"Hey, yourself." Grant pulled her close and kissed her cheek.

"Hi, Kyle," Kira said. She took off the little boy's hat and started to unzip his coat. "He looks just like you, Grant. He has your eyes."

"You think so?"

"Absolutely. Mary Lou must be having a ball with him."

"They are spoiling him rotten." Grant chuckled. "They are the classic doting grandparents."

"He's so lucky to have them. Come on in. Jared, get some toys out so you can play with Kyle. Just remember, he's a lot younger than you."

"Okay, Mom." Jared ran off.

After coats were off and hung up, they made their way to the living room. Kyle seemed to be in awe of the Christmas tree. He kept touching the branches and laughing.

Kira smiled. "Don't you have one at home for him?"

"No." Grant gave her a sheepish grin. "In the rush I forgot to get one."

Kira laughed. "What are you doing tomorrow?"

"We haven't planned that far ahead. I'm sure I'll stop by my parents' house at some point, but nothing's been set in stone. Sam and Brandon have girlfriends now, so they're both traveling out of state. Mom always volunteers to serve Christmas dinner at the senior center in town."

Grant watched Kyle and Jared playing. They were getting along very well. Jared was showing Kyle his Matchbox cars. He didn't seem to have any sensory issues with sharing.

"Just make sure he doesn't put anything in his mouth," Kira told Jared. "We don't want him to choke if the wheels fall off."

"Okay, Mom." Jared turned back to the toys.

"Grant?" Kira paused. She looked so beautiful. But he was afraid of what she might be about to say.

"I wanted to talk to you. I let it go a week, but that was too long." She took a deep breath.

Grant moved closer to her on the couch, reached for her hands, and watched her intently.

Kira closed her eyes as if to gather her thoughts. "You know that the whole time we've been dating, I've struggled with stuff from my past. I . . . I pushed you away at every turn because I was fearful of what would happen to you—to me—to us." She sighed. "I'm probably not even saying this right."

"You're doing fine. Just keep going."

"You were right the other day. I did allow Patrick's memory to stay wedged between us. I let those bad times from the past creep into the present. I'm sorry. I don't want that between us. I only want you." Her voice wavered and he watched a lone tear run down her cheek. "I want you here beside me. I love you. This past week has been truly awful without hearing your voice, without seeing you."

"I love you, Kira." Grant drew her close and claimed her lips. Their tongues entwined, teasing each other, demanding more. Kira's fingers raked through his hair at the nape of his neck as she pulled him closer, her passion matching his.

"Da da?"

Separating from Kira, Grant looked down at Kyle. "Yes, my son?"

"Pooh?"

"He's in the bag." Grant gave Kira another sheepish grin and got up to retrieve Kyle's favorite bear.

Kira laughed. "Welcome to the world of children. Speaking of which, are you going to tell me how Kyle came to be with you?"

Grant grinned again. "I'd rather save that for another time and finish what we started."

"But I don't think now's the time." Kira looked pointedly at Kyle and Jared.

"Yeah, I know. But a man can hope." Grant sighed and settled next to her on the couch.

Kira snuggled close and took his hand. "So, tell me."

"Well, I left the workshop that day and drove straight to New York to see Sophia. She was a little surprised to see me, to say the least. Basically, the short of it is, I told her I wanted to see Kyle, and after seeing him for a little bit and getting a chance to play with him, I told her I wanted custody. She didn't even tend to him. She had an au pair."

"And that was it—she just handed him over?" Kira looked up at Grant.

"Well, not quite that quickly, but yes, basically. She stewed about it for the first day or so, and then she called. She had gotten a job offer in Paris. Basically it wasn't convenient for her to have a child right now so she handed him over. I had the lawyers draw up the custody papers as soon as I got Kyle home. She signed them before she flew off."

Grant smiled down at Kira. "In the end it was that plain and simple. When she gets back she can have visitation at my discretion. That's if she really wants it, which I hardly doubt she will. It's all quite sad, actually."

"Wow. So you are now a full-time dad. How do you like it so far?"

"It's hard work, but I love it. He's incredible. I wanted to tell you about him right away. But you took so long to call. I wanted to share so much with you, Kira." Grant kissed her forehead. "Do you realize that? You were the first one I needed to tell this to and I couldn't."

"You couldn't only because you had laid out the ultimatum," Kira said.

"Yeah, I know."

"Stubborn fool."

Grant laughed. "Tell me something I don't know."

Kira squeezed his hand tightly. "Why don't you and Kyle stay here tonight? I can put you both up in the guest room. Then Kyle will have the tree in the morning with Jared. Jared has presents for you. But I don't have anything for Kyle. I would just need to run out and get him something."

"You don't need to."

"Of course I do. I'm sure Barb won't mind watching the boys, if you want to help me find something. Then we can stop by your place and pick up your presents and pack up Kyle's pajamas and get some more diapers." Kira watched Grant. "What do you think?"

"I think it's a great plan."

"I'll go talk to Barb. She's wrapping presents in her room."

As Kira went off to arrange everything with Barbara, Grant talked with the boys. Kyle was so enthralled with Jared, he was happy to stay and play. Kira returned, ready to go, with Barbara in tow. She was clearly thrilled to watch the boys.

"Jared, we're leaving for a little while," Kira said. "Barbara will be watching you and Kyle. Kyle, this is Barbara."

As Grant watched, Kyle scrambled after Jared, who rushed to Barb. Christmas was almost here.

Chapter 27

After picking up a few gifts for Kyle, they stopped to grab Grant's presents. They packed a duffle bag with overnight clothes and toiletries and then headed back to Kira's house.

As they removed their coats, they were delighted by the aroma of freshly baked cookies. Kira inhaled deeply. "Smells like Barbara kept the boys busy."

"I hope they need a taste-tester." Grant grinned.

They headed to the kitchen. Kira surveyed the scene. Barbara was teaching Kyle to frost sugar cookies with a plastic knife. His face had frosting splattered over it; he appeared to be thoroughly enjoying his task.

Jared was busy applying sprinkles to the frosted cookies.

"Well, isn't this a sight for sore eyes?" Kira exclaimed.

"Cookie." Kyle held up a cookie.

"Do you want one, Mom?" Jared asked. Kira quickly thought back to the previous Christmas, when he had only talked with signs. His verbal skills had improved so much this year, and just like the Early Invention team had expected, his signing had decreased.

"Of course. They look delicious."

"Hey! What about me?" Grant wiped frosting off Kyle's cheek, sending Kyle into giggles.

"The boys have been busy making cookies to leave out for Santa," Barbara explained.

"How will Santa know Kyle is here?" Jared asked.

"You can write him a note and leave it for him by the stockings," Kira answered. "I'll help you if you would like."

"Okay." Jared, relieved, went back to his task of decorating the cookies.

Snagging samples, Kira and Grant set about making their own preparations for Christmas Eve. Kira was especially fond of Christmas now that she had a child of her own. It always had the potential to be a tough holiday for Jared because of the chances of overstimulation, but he had adjusted well over the years. She had been diligent in making sure he received enough sensory therapy to be able to handle the changes in routine to effectively maintain his sense of balance. Christmas brought to Kira a sense of freedom, a sense of childlike abandonment that she relished. She cherished the one day of the year she could get up early with Jared and act like a child herself, enjoying the joy on Jared's face when he opened his presents.

This year would be doubly enjoyable with Grant and Kyle here. She felt giddy with excitement. She giggled as she wondered how Grant felt about getting up at four in the morning to open presents.

"What's so funny?" Grant asked.

"What time do you usually get up on Christmas morning?" Kira asked.

"The normal time, I guess."

"Normal time, what is that? It's Christmas!"

Grant smiled. "Your house, your rules. Okay, tell me. What time are we getting up tomorrow?"

"Well . . . it only comes once a year." Kira smiled back and started playing with the presents under the tree. She found one with her name on it and shook it. "It's from Barbara. What do you think? Gloves?"

"You're worse than a kid. Put that back." Grant laughed.

"Anyway, my rules are that any time after midnight is fair game."

"You're kidding, right?"

"Nope, not kidding." Kira grinned. "But Jared usually gets up about four. If I had my way, we'd be up about two or three."

"You're insane, woman."

"It's once a year. It's Christmas."

Grant shook his head. Kira walked over and curled up next to him on the couch. "It's my absolute favorite time of the year. I love buying presents for other people. Of course, there is always the getting of gifts. But there is just something magical about Christmas."

Grant pulled her close. "You're beautiful. Insane, but beautiful."

Kira settled in. For the first time in years, she felt a sense of calm. For once she didn't have any doubts. Her mind was free and clear with peace and joy at being at Grant's side.

"Mom, I'm ready for your help with Santa's letter." Jared came in carrying paper and a pen. Kyle toddled after him with paper and a crayon.

"Are you going to write to Santa, too?" Grant asked Kyle.

Kyle nodded yes with great enthusiasm. Both boys sprawled on the floor to write their letters. Kira helped Jared with the words when he needed them. Kyle scribbled with his crayon. Kira's heart swelled with love as she watched the two boys. This was the family she had always wanted.

After the boys were done, Kira got out the stockings she had prepared earlier for Grant and Kyle. Grant helped Kyle hang his next to Jared's. They placed his drawing in it for Santa. Grant hung his stocking next to Kira's. Kira hummed Christmas tunes as she took pictures.

Finally putting the camera down, Kira turned to Grant. "I'm going to set up the guest room bed. I imagine we'll need to get the boys in bed early."

"Yeah, because someone will have them up at an ungodly hour." Grant winked.

"Hey, Jared wakes me up. Don't you think Kyle will be awake, all excited, wondering if Santa has been here yet?" Kira laughed as she walked down the hallway to prepare the guest room.

* * *

Settling the boys down after a quick dinner of turkey burgers, carrot sticks, and oven fries was no easy feat. Kyle was wound up from all the Christmas preparations and talk of Santa. Jared, taxed by the change of routine of having Kyle and Grant sleep over, started to slip away. Kira guided him into her bedroom to do sensory therapy in a quiet space. After deep joint compressions and sensory stimulation, Jared was once again more focused and able to talk with his mother.

Kira said, "Jared, I know you usually have a tough time around Christmas, but tonight seems a little tougher. What's going on?"

"Kyle is loud."

"Well, he's just a little boy. When kids are little like that, they get excited. And sometimes loud."

Jared scratched the back of his neck. "Why is he spending the night?"

"I invited them to stay over so they could share our tree. You understand that Kyle is Grant's son, right?"

"Yes."

"Well, Kyle just moved in with Grant last week. His mom had to move away for her work. Grant was so busy fixing up a room for Kyle, he forgot to get a Christmas tree."

"Oh." Kira could see that Jared was quietly absorbing this news.

She continued, "I thought we could share our Christmas tree with them. Now Santa can leave presents for Kyle under our tree. You would want your presents under a Christmas tree, right?"

"Right. And I wanted Grant here. I just don't know about Kyle. He's loud!"

"Okay. Fair enough. But what can we do so it's not too loud for you?" Kira asked.

"Can I wear my headphones?" Jared went over to his desk and got them. "Ms. Cheryl lets me wear these when it's loud."

"Good idea. And you two boys are going to bed pretty soon anyway."

"Okay, Mom." Jared hugged her. He put on his headphones.

"You need to tell me if you need more sensory therapy."

"Yup."

Heading back for the living room, Kira stopped Kyle as he tried to grab Jared's headphones. "No, Kyle. Those are Jared's. You can't have those."

"Me."

"No, you go find another toy. Jared needs those now." Kira took his hand and led him into the living room.

"Is everything okay?" Grant asked.

"Me," Kyle said, pouting.

"You what?" Grant asked.

"He wants Jared's headphones, but Jared needs them to block out the noise right now. He's a little overloaded because it's louder tonight with a toddler in the house, and he's not used to it," Kira explained.

"Kyle, let's find another toy. You can't have those." Grant was firm and distracted Kyle immediately.

Kira mouthed a thank you to Grant over Kyle's head.

"Kira, this is Jared's house, and Kyle will have to learn that Jared's needs must come first with regard to his autism. It will just become a fact of life for Kyle. He will learn."

"You ready to try to get these guys into bed?" Kira asked.

"Absolutely." Grant picked up Kyle and his Pooh bear. "Come on, you, time for bed."

"Jared, bedtime," Kira said.

Kira and Grant, with Kyle in tow, went to Jared's room first. As Jared rearranged the stuffed animals on his bed, he asked, "Do you think Santa will bring me the rocking horse, Mom?"

"I don't know, Jared. We'll see in the morning." Kira kissed him. "Come wake me when you get up. No going to the living room first, and don't wake Kyle."

"I know. 'Night, Grant. 'Night, Kyle." Jared blew kisses.

"'Night, Jared." Grant kissed him. "Sweet dreams."

"Sleep?" Kyle pointed to Jared's bed.

"No, Kyle. You're not sleeping with Jared. You'll see him in the morning," Grant said.

Moving on to the guest room, Grant tucked Kyle into the queen size bed they would share. They had pushed the bed against a wall, and Grant had lined up the kitchen chairs as a barrier on the other side. Kyle snuggled right down with his Pooh bear.

"'Night, Kyle." Kira leaned over and kissed him. Kyle hugged her tight.

"'Night, son. Daddy will be right back. You stay in bed." Grant kissed him.

Kira headed for the living room while Grant stood in the doorway of the bedroom to make sure Kyle stayed put. Clearly exhausted from his day, the toddler drifted off to sleep almost immediately.

Kira picked up toys scattered about the living room as she waited for Grant to come back. After picking up all the toys, she got out the stocking stuffers and proceeded to fill stockings. She heard the spare room door shut softly just as she filled the last stocking. Grant went out to his car and returned with the rocking horse that he had crafted. It was beautiful. She had not seen it with the polyurethane coating. It shined.

She got out her camera and took pictures while Grant set up a workbench for Kyle from Santa.

"That's adorable," Kira said.

"I thought Kyle would like it. He's always banging things."

"Then he really must be your son," Kira laughed. "Oh, look, it has a little tool belt. They make the cutest things now."

Once everything was done for Christmas Eve, Kira and Grant sat back on the couch and surveyed the living room. Barbara had excused herself after dinner to watch *It's a Wonderful Life* in her room. Kira knew that she had also made arrangements to help Grant's parents with the senior Christmas lunch.

Admiring the filled stockings and the presents under the tree, Kira sighed. The boys would certainly have a good Christmas morning. Then she felt a pang of longing. It was if they were a family. How she wished it were true.

"You okay?" Grant asked.

"Yeah, why?" Kira looked at him, surprised.

"A funny look crossed your face."

"I get kind of sentimental, I guess, around Christmas. That's all." She shrugged.

Grant pulled her close. He ran his fingers along her jaw line. "I have missed you. I'm so sorry we were apart."

"Me too, Grant. I wish we hadn't fought." She looked into his blue eyes, trying to read them. They seemed much bluer tonight, so serious.

"Kira, I love you," Grant whispered as he moved toward her, his lips softly brushing hers. Her lips parted slightly in response.

"I love you, Grant," Kira whispered. He nibbled the side of her neck, shifting to her earlobe. His lips slowly moved down the angle of her jaw, stopping just at the edge of her mouth. She turned her face slightly, and kissed him. Her hand reached up behind his neck and pulled him closer. The passion between them ignited, leaving both of them wanting more as Grant broke off the kiss.

"Is something wrong?" Kira asked.

"No. I just . . . God, Kira, I want to make sure I do this right this time."

"What do you mean?" Kira asked.

Grant suddenly stood up and said, "I'm going to bed." He bent down and kissed her gently again. "I love you. I'll see you in the morning."

"Grant?"

"In the morning." Then he quickly left the room.

Chapter 28

Kira tossed and turned all night. Why had Grant left the room so abruptly? The passion was there, no doubt about that. They were good together. Still, she knew he needed to work through the recent issues with Sophia and the discovery of his son. Finally, it seemed like Charlene had brought some good into their lives—even if her intentions had been exactly the opposite. Now Kira just needed the patience to help Grant adjust.

Four in the morning. She sighed. It wouldn't be long before—

The door opened a crack. Jared's head poked through.

"Merry Christmas, Jared."

"Mom, can we get up?" Jared bounded across the room and jumped on the bed.

Kira pulled him close. "Can't we sleep a little longer?" She laughed. "It's still early."

"Mom, it's Christmas. I want to see if Santa came!" Jared bounced on the bed. "Come on."

"Okay, okay. Stop bouncing." Kira pushed him over with a pillow. She stood up and reached for her bathrobe. "We'll have to go get the rest of the sleepyheads."

"Let's go." Jared raced for the guest room.

"Wait." Kira hurried after him, tying the belt on her robe. "Open the door quietly."

Jared and Kira peeked into the spare room. She saw that Grant and Kyle were still sleeping. Kira motioned with her fingers: one, two, three. "Merry Christmas!" they said in unison.

Grant picked his head up and looked at the clock. He groaned. "You two are nuts."

Kira laughed as Jared ran and jumped on Grant. "Get up, Grant. It's Christmas!"

Kyle woke next. At first his eyes grew large as if he'd been startled, but seeing the fun that Jared was having, he sat up and flung himself across Grant's face. Grant's voice was muffled. "There'd better be coffee ready."

"Coffee? On Christmas?" Kira motioned the boys to move. Then she ambushed Grant with a pillow in the face. "Merry Christmas!"

"You wait." Grant was quick. Grabbing the pillow behind him with one hand and Kira's wrist with the other, he planted the pillow against her shoulder. The boys howled with laughter on the other side of the bed, watching the adults have their pillow fight.

Kira and Grant, exchanging glances, nodded and then attacked the boys. With squeals of laughter, Jared and Kyle couldn't fight back.

"Does anyone want coffee in this ruckus?" Barbara asked from the doorway. Kira looked over. "Did we wake you?"

"No, honey. I have been up waiting for Jared to come get me. But then I heard the commotion and realized I would have to come join the fun." She laughed. "All the noise certainly sounds good."

"Merry Christmas, Barbara." Grant stood up, straightened his red pajama bottoms, slipped a T-shirt over his head, and went over to give her a kiss on the cheek. "Coffee sounds wonderful. Certainly much better than a pillow in the face."

Barbara smirked. "Maybe it was what you deserved, sleeping so late."

Grant feigned being upset. "You don't mean that."

"Can we open our presents now?" Jared asked.

"Of course. But wait, I have to turn on the lights," Kira said.

"Already done," Barb said. "I had to do something productive while I waited for you monkeys in here."

Kira laughed. "Monkeys? Our pillow fight was very civil."

"And when was the last time you did that?" Barb asked.

"I honestly couldn't tell you, but it was fun."

Kira picked up Kyle, reached for the diaper bag, and changed his diaper.

"I can do that," Grant said.

"I know, but I don't mind." She smiled down at Kyle. "Think Santa came, Kyle?"

"Santa." Kyle grinned.

"Let's go see."

Kira put Kyle down and he ran over to take Jared's hand. "Come on, Jared!"

"Go ahead, you two." She nodded.

The boys ran down the hallway with the adults following close behind.

Jared stopped short when he got to the living room. Kira snatched her camera from the hall table and scooted around to get in front of him to snap pictures of his expression.

"Told you, Mom! Santa brought me the horse!" He walked over to it slowly. First he ran his hands over it and then he walked around it. Finally he sat on it, gripped the handles near the horse's ears, and started rocking. "It's just what I wanted."

Kira, still snapping pictures, smiled. "I'm glad you got it, Jared. It's beautiful."

"Santa makes them," Jared proclaimed.

"He certainly does," she said.

Kyle spotted the tool bench and ran to it. "Me!"

"Yes, Kyle. Santa gave that to you," Grant said.

Kira took pictures of Kyle as he banged with his new hammer. She backed up and was able to include both boys, engrossed with their gifts. Grant sat on the floor beside Kyle, showing him all the gadgets involved in the tool bench.

"What a scene, Barb." Kira sighed as she settled on the couch.

"Well, you look happy," Barb observed.

"Does it get any better than this?"

"I wouldn't think so. What's better than being surrounded by your family on a holiday?" Barb spoke softly.

Kira looked at her. "My family," she repeated.

Barbara nodded.

Kira took Barbara's hand. "And you know that includes you."

The volume of the noise suddenly soared to the rafters as Kyle picked up the hammer again.

"I'll have to get Jared's headphones," she told Barb. "But first, maybe we can distract them."

"Who's ready for stockings?" Kira asked.

Both boys, too busy with their gifts from Santa, ignored her.

"I could go for that coffee now." Grant laughed. "Looks like we might actually have a few minutes while they play with these toys."

"Yeah. You realize present opening usually drags out a couple of hours," Kira said. "I'll get the coffee."

"I'll help you. Barb, you want a cup?" Grant asked.

"I'd love one. It's a gift just to sit here and be waited on." Barb smiled. "And I love watching the boys enjoy their presents."

"It's my pleasure to get it for you. Enjoy the boys," Grant said.

Grant followed Kira to the kitchen. She began to fill three cups with coffee.

"You okay?" he asked.

"Just tired. I didn't sleep well."

"I'm sorry." He pulled her close. "I hope it wasn't because of the way I ended things last night."

She looked up at him. "What happened? I wanted you, Grant."

"I wanted you, too. It's just . . . I figured it was probably best to be there with Kyle. This is all so new to him. And he was in a strange bed."

Kira sensed that there was more to it, but she let it go for now. They had both been under so much stress lately.

There was no point starting a quarrel on Christmas morning.

"How does Barb take her coffee?" Grant asked.

"Black."

"I really do love you, Kira." Grant pulled her close and kissed her. "We need to talk later. How about a walk on the beach? Back to where we took that first walk."

"Sounds good. A nice cold walk!" Kira shook her head at Grant and made a face.

Grant chuckled. "I'll keep you warm, I promise."

"I'll hold you to that." Kira picked up her coffee and started back to the living room as Grant followed behind with cups for him and Barbara.

The rest of the morning flew as the boys opened presents and their stockings. Kira enjoyed watching Jared take Kyle under his wing. Kyle was watching Jared for cues, and they were really acting like brothers.

"Open my present next." Jared handed her a tiny gift. "Grant helped me when we went shopping."

"I remember. And you never told me what it was," Kira said.

"I kept a secret."

"Good for you, Jared."

Kira's eyes filled with tears when she opened the tiny box and found a pair of dangly earrings inside. They were made up of three white balls on wire hoops.

"Jared, they're beautiful. I love them." She hugged Jared close. Then she turned to Grant. "Thank you, Grant, for helping him."

"I didn't do anything, really. Jared knew exactly what he wanted. I simply took him to the store."

Kira kissed Jared on the forehead. "I love them so much, Jared. Thank you." She slipped them onto her ears, lifting her dishelved hair so he could see.

Kira's spirits continued to rise when Grant proclaimed that he loved the shirts from her and Jared. Barbara was thrilled with her new cookbooks and cashmere sweater.

As the boys continued to play with their gifts, Kira went around picking up empty boxes and wrapping paper. What a morning it had been. She loved Christmas, but it always went so quickly.

Grant said, "I should call Mom and Dad. Do you mind if I phone from your room to get out of the noise?"

"Of course not. You don't need to ask," Kira said.

"They will be expecting to see us, at some point."

"Of course. I knew you and Kyle would be going over there tonight."

"I don't think you understood what I said."

"What?"

"I said they will be expecting *us*."

"I heard you."

"Kira. They will be expecting *us*. Me, Kyle, you, and Jared. And Barb, if she wants to go."

Tears formed in Kira's eyes as she smiled. She wiped her eyes on the sleeve of her bathrobe. "Why am I so teary today? Grant, of course we'll go."

She sat back on the couch as Grant left the room to call his parents. Five minutes later, he came back to the living room door and gestured for her to take the phone.

"Me?" Kira mouthed to Grant.

He just grinned and pressed the phone into her hand.

"Merry Christmas, Mary Lou," Kira said.

"Merry Christmas to you. I understand you had a houseful this morning."

"Yes. It was wonderful; the boys are still enjoying it," Kira said as she watched the boys playing.

"That's why I wanted to talk to you. It seems ridiculous to tear them away from their new toys. If you don't mind, Marcus and I would like to bring their presents to your house tonight."

"Of course, I don't mind. In fact, Barb and I had planned on a small turkey for dinner, but I'm sure there's enough for everyone. Why don't you come for dinner when the senior lunch is through?"

"I'll help, Kira," Grant said in the background.

"There. Grant's saying he will help too. It's all set, Mary Lou. If Sam and Brandon come back in time, bring them along also," Kira said.

"That sounds great. We'll follow Barb home after the senior lunch. And, Kira?"

"Yes?"

"I'm so glad we'll be seeing you today. We've missed you." With a soft click, Mary Lou was gone.

Kira turned to Grant. "Well, your parents will be joining us for dinner after the senior lunch. Maybe the boys if they're back, too."

Grant frowned.

"Aren't you pleased that they're coming?"

"Of course I am. But I had forgotten about the senior lunch. Barb will have to leave in a while." Then his face brightened as he looked at the clock. "Actually, it's still pretty early since we got up before the crack of dawn." He reached for her hand. "Let's get dressed and take that walk while she's still here."

Chapter 29

They started down the walkway toward the beach. Kira breathed in deeply, enjoying the salt air. She hadn't had the chance to walk along the beach in a while.

"I love this. I used to be out here daily," Kira said.

"I remember. Have you been too busy with the new job?"

"I guess so. But I'll have to remember to make time for it again. I just feel so relaxed now. It's amazing how the sound of the waves and the smell of the salt air has that effect on me." Kira breathed in deeply again and closed her eyes.

A moment later, she opened them again and continued walking. Looping her arm through Grant's, she looked up at him. "So, what is it we need to talk about?"

"Well, you jump right to it." Grant chuckled.

"Did you want to make small talk?" Kira mocked. "So, how's the weather? Seems pretty darn chilly to me."

"Wise guy."

Kira giggled. "That's Ms. Wise guy to you. But seriously, Grant, what's going on? Do you want to explain to me what happened last night?"

Grant stared out at the ocean as he slowed his pace. Kira stopped walking and watched him. She waited patiently for him to speak again. He finally said, "It's like I said last night. I just want to get things right. There are some things I've been wanting to say to you."

"Okay." Kira waited.

"Kira," Grant turned and faced her, "I know that things between us the last few weeks have been a little up in the air. I take most of that responsibility because I put the ultimatum to you. The news about Kyle and Sophia really caught me off guard. And then when you thought I had simply abandoned them—"

"Grant, I didn't know what to think," Kira interrupted.

"I realize that now. In fact, we both should have known that if Charlene was involved, it was a bad situation to begin with. We shouldn't have attacked each other." Grant paused and looked at the ocean again. He seemed to be gathering his thoughts.

Kira wondered what was going through his mind. Where was he going with all this?

He reached for her hand. "I don't know how to say any of this, it seems. Kira, there have been times you pushed me away because you didn't know how I would react. But I won't run out on you. All I can say is I love you."

"I love you, too, Grant."

He ran his free hand through his hair. "Kira, I meant what I said before about there being an *us*." Grant grabbed both her hands. "Are you ready to be a family? Is that what you want?"

Kira's heart seemed to skip a beat. "I think so," she whispered. "But Grant, is that really what you want?"

"More than anything in this world. I want you. I want to share my life with you. I want to have a family with you. I want to raise our sons together." Grant dropped to one knee in the cold damp sand in front of Kira. "Kira Nichols, would you do me the honor of becoming my wife?"

Kira's eyes widened. She couldn't believe it. She heard the sound of her heartbeat in her ears. She felt her eyes pool with tears, which threatened to spill over her lashes as she smiled and nodded.

"Yes, yes," Kira whispered and then shouted. She leaped into his arms and wrapped her legs around him. "I love you."

He kissed her. "We may need a bigger house, you know," Grant said.

"I know."

"How do you feel about the oceanfront property next door?" Grant slowly lowered her to the ground. "Maybe Barbara could phone up her sisters and they could all move into yours."

Kira looked into Grant's eyes and smiled. "I love the house next door, especially knowing that you built it and it brought us all together."

"Good. I want to stay close so you can still have your daily walks on the beach."

"Thank you. And maybe one day the boys can make their own tree house with their dad."

Grant pulled her close. "God, I couldn't love you more."

"I love you." She took his hand as the waved crashed onto the shore behind them. "Come on. Let's go tell our family about the wedding."

Made in the USA
Columbia, SC
31 October 2020